The Bully's Milky Roommate

Jade Swallow

Copyright © 2025 by Jade Swallow

All rights reserved.

No part of this book may be reproduced in any form or by any electronic or mechanical means, including information storage and retrieval systems, without written permission from the author, except for the use of brief quotations in a book review.

Contents

Content Warnings	v
1. Katie	1
2. Bryan	12
3. Katie	26
4. Bryan	39
5. Katie	48
6. Bryan	55
7. Katie	63
8. Bryan	70
About the Author	79
Also by Jade Swallow	81

Content Warnings

This book contains a forbidden erotic relationship between two consenting adults and is intended for readers over 18. That being said, this book appeals to very specific tastes, and some of the content mentioned may be triggering.

A non-exhaustive list of content includes: A forbidden relationship with a bully, lactation kink with loads of filthy milking, breeding kink (unprotected sex), a sexual relationship between roommates, oral sex, dirty talking, pregnancy, pregnant sex (with a baby bump), steamy scenes in public, sneaking around, and typos and grammatical errors.

Please note this is a work of fiction featuring imaginary scenarios. Only read if you are comfortable with the above themes. The author does not endorse the beliefs or actions of the characters.

If you read this book anywhere other than Amazon, you have an illegal pirated copy. I encourage you to research the harmful effects of piracy on authors and obtain a legal copy instead. Thanks.

v

Chapter 1
Katie

"I can't be roommates with Bryan Livingston! There's gotta be a mistake." I stand in Heathcliff Academy's dorm office, my hands on my hips. Dressed in a loose hoodie that hides my milky problem, and a pair of jeans, I'm grasping at straws. It's my final year at Heathcliff Academy and I hoped for peace this year. However, when I walked into my room to find my bully lounging on my bed with that sexy smirk on his face, all thoughts of a normal senior year dissolved like soap bubbles. "Aren't boys supposed to be assigned to the boy's dorm?"

My fingers are white as they clutch the edge of the desk, gazing down at a raven-haired administrator who furiously types away at her computer. Her name is Saumya and I've seen her at the office before. I've been going to Heathcliff Academy for two years now. My Dad is an investment banker who works in Switzerland and my parents live there with my younger brother. They want me to get into an Ivy League college, which is why they sent me to Heathcliff, a school with an illustrious track record of getting students into top colleges. However, from the moment I started school, my life's been on a slippery slope. On my very first day, I caught the attention of Bryan Livingston, one of the kings of Heathcliff Academy. He hails from one of the richest and most influential old-money families in America and has the whole school eating out of the palm of his hand.

Footsteps resound on the polished wooden floor of the 100-year-old building I'm standing in, and I don't even have to glance back to see who it is.

"Are you complaining about being my roommate, cupcake?" Bryan's voice is deep and rich, inciting a mix of fear and something primal deep in my belly. My nose scrunches at his use of that pet name. He's been calling me 'cupcake' ever since he found me eating a cupcake, the icing on my face, during my first week here. I hate the sound of it because it reminds me of all that I've had to go through because of him.

"It looks like there's been a mistake." Saumya looks up right in time to save me. Bryan comes to stand next to me and when his hand comes to rest on my hip, holding me like I'm his girl, my pussy clenches in response. Damn, my traitorous body. My nipples begin to tingle, reminding me why it's such a bad idea to share a room with him. If he ever finds out that I'm producing milk, my high school life will be over. I can already imagine how everyone will call me a cow and moo at me whenever I enter a room. It's already bad enough because I'm curvy and overweight, something that my classmates take a jab at every now and then. Bryan calling me 'cupcake' only makes things worse for me because the others are always asking if I've eaten my daily cupcake yet. Mom says I have attractiveness hidden under the layers of fat and blonde hair, but I have yet to see it.

Fear pulses through my aching chest at the thought of being roommates with my bully.

The Bully's Milky Roommate

Bryan's bright green eyes turn to me, evil and smoldering at the same time. With his tall, slightly muscular build, he looks like a jock. Bryan plays football for the school, which is one of the reasons he's popular among the girls. The thing I don't understand is why he's obsessed with me. He never misses a chance to touch me or put his arm around me, like I'm his toy to play with. Does he enjoy staking a claim on me?

"It looks like we assigned Bryan to your room because no others were available." Saumya's dark eyes are apologetic. "It looks like the system classified Bryan as a girl."

Bryan frowns and though that's funny, I don't dare smile. His hand squeezes my hip and my heavy tits ache with the need to be pumped. A week ago, I found out that my breasts are producing milk. It was horrifying so I rushed to the doctor right away. She told me due to a hormonal imbalance, I was lactating and I would be fine in a few weeks. I just needed to pump regularly and take the medication she gave me. However, one week later, my problem showed no sign of going away. Bryan Livingston's taunts are the last thing I need.

"That's too bad." Bryan turns his charming smile to Saumya, something he saves for people he wants to get to do his bidding. "You know, I quite like my roommate. Katie and I will get along quite well. After all, we're really good friends. Isn't that right, cupcake?"

The malice in his gaze when he looks at me doesn't go unnoticed. Hell no. I can't let this happen.

"No!" I cut in, pulling my body away from Bryan's. He flashes me an annoyed look, telling me I'm going to pay for it later. "I need my own room. Can't you find another room for Bryan? There's got to be a free spot in the boy's dorm."

Saumya types away, checking for empty spots. "I'm

sorry, all the rooms are full right now. That's why the system put Bryan in your room. I'll talk to the manager and try to get this sorted, but you guys are going to have to stay together for the time being."

"How long is it going to take?" I ask, already worried. The freedom that I wanted is slipping through my fingers, and I don't know how I'm going to last even a week with Bryan without exposing my secret.

"A few weeks, at least." Saumya gives me an apologetic look. "I'm so sorry about this, Katie. I'll find a way to get you into your own room as soon as possible."

* * *

Many hours later, I'm busy at work on my sewing machine in my new room. I unpacked and decorated my side of the room. Bryan's unpacked belongings lie on his single bed, which looks a little larger than mine. His desk is overflowing with books and stationery while mine is neatly organized. After my trip to the dorm office, I went to class and then, came back to pump and finish my homework.

Bryan and I share a room with an en-suite bathroom, which unfortunately means he's going to smell my milk in there. I've got to be careful when I pump and air out the bathroom soon after. Though we're stuck together, I'm determined to keep my secret.

Bryan has football practice in the evenings, which means I get to have some time to myself. The last rays of twilight filter through my room window, illuminating the dress I'm working on. I sew in the evenings and it brings me a lot of peace to work on my designs.

My hands stop on the sewing machine. A fluffy, blue dress hangs out of my sewing machine, half-stitched.

The Bully's Milky Roommate

Gorgeous layers of satin and tulle complete the skirt. I've been working on the dress for a while now. When I close my eyes, I can imagine myself looking like a princess in that blue gown at prom. Though I know I'm going to be alone at prom, it doesn't stop me from fantasizing about wearing a beautiful, sequined gown that I designed for the most eventful event in my high school career. Next to me is a sketch I made. Pulling off the pin cushion on my wrist, I stare at the beaded, off-shoulder bodice. I've always liked making my own clothes since the clothes that fit others don't really look good on me. I lean back against the seat, dreaming of the day when I get to graduate and go out into the world, ready to pursue my dream. I haven't told mom and dad yet because they want me to go to college. But I want to be a fashion designer and open my own line of plus-size couture someday. I've even applied to a few apprenticeships with designers I admire in New York City. But nothing's materialized yet. Of course, I could totally do those apprenticeships without my parents' permission, since I am an adult now, but I want to get my high school diploma first.

I gaze down at my breasts which are starting to fill up already. Maybe I can pump once more after Bryan goes to bed. After Saumya's disappointing revelation, I went to class, but I couldn't focus all day. My tits hurt every time I move and the way my pussy gets damp whenever I'm filled with milk is a huge problem. So far, I've been making myself come to breeding kink porn. Nothing turns me on like a thick, big cock breeding my pussy. I know it's weird and shameful, especially because I'm only eighteen and have no desire to have kids in school.

However, once I discovered the rabbit hole of breeding kink, there was no stopping my descent into darkness. I love how curvy pregnancy makes a woman, how it makes it okay to be soft and curvy and big. Before I discovered porn, I didn't even know men liked curvy and pregnant women. I've always been insecure about my curvy, short frame, but watching pregnancy and breeding porn makes me feel better about my body. However, with Bryan living with me, masturbating to my secret stash is going to be hard.

The door opens and I barely have time to collect my thoughts before Bryan walks in. He looks all sweaty and sexy in a pair of joggers that show off his thick thighs and a tight, gray t-shirt that clings to his rock-solid chest. He's broad and big, filled with muscles where I'm all fat and curves. I exhale sharply, ignoring the way my core clenches with lust when he walks in. He's like those big, strong men in the porn I watch, virility radiating from him in waves. He's an alpha in every way, his chiseled jaw, straight nose, and those dark, full lips completing the picture. Behind him, I hear a gaggle of females, screaming and sighing as he walks inside and shuts the door. He's been living in the girl's dorm for a day and he's already so popular.

Bryan bolts the door shut, shaking his head. "The perils of being popular. I feel so welcome at the girl's dorm. Maybe I'll stay here all year."

I scoff. "Don't even dream about it."

Too late, I realize that Bryan's eyes are on me. His jaw parts slightly and I realize what he's seeing. I stand up jerkily, pulling the gown I'm sewing away from the machine and dumping it onto the bed. However, before I can grab the sketch, Bryan picks it up, gazing at it.

"What is this? A prom dress?" His eyes study my carefully crafted masterpiece, moving between the sketch and the dress on my bed. Under it is my signature. God, I've never regretted this as much as I do now. "You design dresses." I jump up, trying to grab my sketch from him, but he raises his hand over his head, moving it away from my grasp.

"Give it back. It's mine."

"You want to be a fashion designer." His words hit me straight in the gut. God, how did I fail to take into account Bryan's reaction when he realizes I make my own dresses? Of course, he's going to give me a snide remark about how I'm too big for any decent dress sold at the department store. But that isn't even the worst part. The worst part is that he took one look at my sketch and recognized my dreams while my parents have no idea that fashion is more than a 'hobby' to me. "I'm right, aren't I?" He takes another look at the sketch and nods his head. "Is that dress for you?"

I freeze mid-way, not knowing how to respond to his remark. Should I admit to it or deny it? Will this be all over school by tomorrow? My cheeks redden with humiliation. I'm not ready for the world to know about my dreams yet.

"It looks like someone unpacked." Bryan whistles, his green gaze moving around the room and getting stuck on my sewing machine. He's at it before I unfreeze my legs, running those long, thick fingers over the surface of my most prized possession. "What do we have here, a sewing machine?" His eyes cut to mine and I wish the ground would open up and swallow me. I lower my shaky fingers, not meeting his eye.

"It's none of your business." I lean forward, my tits still hurting from earlier, drying to pry him away from my sewing machine.

"Whoa, calm your claws, kitten." He grabs my hand and pushes it over my head. Before I know it, I'm pinned against the wall next to my sewing machine, Bryan's body pressing against mine. My sketch flies down, pushed out of

Bryan's grasp. I reach to grab it, but I'm stuck between the wall and Bryan's his fingers holding my wrists together. When I raise my head, my words die on my lips. I stare straight into Bryan's moss-green eyes that suddenly look so much more beautiful. Up close, I can see the stubble dotting his cheek, the way the shadows play on his full lips. The urge to rise to my toes and press my mouth to his makes a flame spark alive inside my core. At once, all the blood in my body rushes between my legs, my heartbeats echoing in slow motion.

"Let me go." My voice is feeble and fragile, devoid of any conviction.

"You're my prisoner, Katie." His whispers light my blood on fire. I can't handle this proximity between us. "I'm never gonna let you go."

"You're a psycho, you know that?" Our eyes meet, a fog of sexual tension choking me.

"Yeah, I know." His voice is low, his body warm and anchoring. If he were some other guy, I'd dream of him railing me against the wall right now. But he's Bryan Livingston, my bully, so I just bite my lower lip until it hurts. "And what you're doing is admirable. Fashion design huh. I never would've thought you were into art. You're always so quiet. I always thought you wanted to go to college like the rest of us. It looks like you've got claws too."

I don't know why his words stroke my confidence. Maybe it's because nobody has ever seen me as someone capable of forging her way in life. Of all the people, I can't believe it's Bryan who is saying those words to me. I squint my eyes, wondering if he's messing with me. "You don't have to play nice with me. I know you hate me."

"I don't hate you." His voice is low and when I feel his hardness pressing against the V of my thighs, I let out an involuntary moan. "I just like playing with you. You always try to fight back, and it makes everything more fun."

"So, I'm just your plaything with a hobby you approve of?" I can't think with him standing so close to me. Desire fuels my veins and if he doesn't back off soon, I might end up kissing him. "You've been targeting me ever since I transferred to Heathcliff. Everyone at school thinks I'm your toy, and they stay away. But you won't even talk to me. You've isolated me from everyone. If that's not hate, I don't know what is."

He grinds his hips into mine, making his desire known. A stab of pleasure runs up my spine when I feel his thickness slip between my legs. We're both covered, but the way he pushes his dick between my pajama-clad legs is heavenly. My body needs the release so bad. "Does that feel like hatred?"

I can't speak. Bryan's masculine scent infiltrates my nose, making me so horny. I want to peel the layers of fabric from my pussy and grind on that thick bulge of his bare. He must be huge, guessing from how he feels. My eyes go dark and I moan when his hips join mine, offering no resistance.

His voice is breathy, his hands squeezing around my wrist.

"I mean it, Katie. Not a lot of kids at our school have dreams that their parents don't approve of. Our futures are set in stone—graduate school, attend college, join the family business, get married to a cold-blooded heiress, pop out three kids, and work till the day you die." His voice sounds on edge when he says that, making me wonder if he wants something different. I shake my head. "I might be your bully, but I recognize talent when I see it."

Talent? He thinks I'm talented? This is a day of surprises.

"You don't really mean that." This is Bryan Livingston, the boy with a golden spoon. What does he even have to complain about? His mom is the head of the board of trustees at Heathcliff Academy. He was pretty much guaranteed a spot here since the day he was born. "You're really good at taking advantage of your status as a Livingston. Why would you even bother about your parents not approving?"

My words are harsh but the way my wet pussy grinds on his cock tells another story. I can't stop myself from responding to him, not when I'm so horny and high-strung.

"Mmmm...." His mouth ghosts over my jaw and I close my eyes, bracing myself for a kiss. I'm caged, a prisoner to his whims. My body needs the pleasure he can give me. I feel liquid trickle down my thighs, my arousal pulsing violently in my belly. I tilt my head, accepting his kiss. Bryan's lips ghost mine, his breath misting against my mouth. Just when I think he's going to put me out of my misery and kiss me, his face pulls away.

"Damn it." He backs away, raking a hand through his hair. His eyes are dark with lust, his cock throbbing, but he won't touch me. That's like a bucket of cold water to my face. What the hell was I thinking, rubbing myself on him like a slut? Of course, Bryan was toying with me. He's my bully. He's got absolutely no tender feelings for me.

Shame washes through my body as I lean forward mindlessly.

My new roommate peels himself off me, leaving my body thrumming with repressed sexual tension. Bryan peels his shirt off, throwing it on the floor before he says, "I'm going to take a shower."

I can't take my eyes off his rippling back muscles, his shoulders so broad and arms so thick. When the bathroom door shuts, I swallow. Gathering my drawing from the floor, I stuff it into my wardrobe with my half-finished dress and sit on my bed, my face in my hands. I'm red with embarrassment, cursing myself out mentally. How could I have fallen for Bryan's trick?

I collapse against the pillow as the sound of shower water fills my ears. Even now, I can't stop thinking about him. I can't stop longing for the kiss that I was denied. When I'm next to Bryan, I feel oddly liberated, like I'm just a mass of desires and longing. I mutter a curse, an uncomfortable realization settling cold in my panicked heart.

I'm attracted to Bryan Livingston. Of all the people in the world, I'm attracted to my bully. Who also happens to be my roommate.

God save me.

Chapter 2
Bryan

Katie Mendelson is the bane of my existence.

I watch my roommate sit in the back seat in class, hiding her body under her loose school uniform. The boys are looking at her, the way they always do, which is why I claimed her the day she came to school. I lean back on my chair, surrounded by cheerleaders who are telling me how excited they are about tomorrow's game. But all I can see is Katie, a strand of her blonde ponytail falling over her magnolia skin. Her cheeks are always flushed, and her round face is so adorable. The uniform does a poor job of hiding those lush curves which drive me insane. Her curvy body is my kryptonite.

The moment I laid eyes on her a year ago, I knew I wanted her. She was all my fantasies rolled into one. With that soft voice and those big blue eyes, she was everything I'd dreamed of in a girl. So, I asked her out during lunch and she flat-out rejected me. I was shocked and kinda embarrassed too. I'd never been turned down by a girl before.

"I...don't want to go out with you. I don't even know

The Bully's Milky Roommate

you." She didn't even meet my eyes as she rejected me. Katie has a habit of avoiding eye contact.

"We could get to know each other," I suggested. "You're new, aren't you?"

She turned away from me, saying she wanted to focus on getting through high school. However, a day later, I saw her talking to one of the boys, giving him the smile that she refused to give me. That's when I decided to settle for revenge. If I couldn't have her, nobody could.

When she appeared in the cafeteria that day with a cupcake, I started calling her cupcake. I put my arm around her and announced to everyone that she was my new plaything and nobody was allowed to be friends with her. She fought me, she resisted, but in the end, my influence won over. My mom's family started Heathcliff Academy, which means I'm virtually royalty here. Nobody would dare go against me. It was only a matter of time before Katie became isolated and everyone started avoiding her.

That's when the bullying started. I always kept my comments direct and cutting, so that she'd never get the wrong idea. Soon, it became clear that I was football royalty and she was just a wallflower, stumbling her way through school. The kids stopped bothering her, and whenever they made fun of her, I was always there to put them in place. My revenge soon became a way to protect the girl I liked, to keep her away from those fat-shaming bastards.

When I turn my head slightly, I notice that Katie's eyes are on me. Instantly, she looks down, not wanting me to know that she's been staring at me. I smile, remembering her sketch from yesterday. When Katie walked into my dorm room last morning, I was shocked. I knew there had been a mistake because I'd been assigned to the girl's dormitory. I had been planning on getting mom to rectify the mistake until Katie walked in. She looked so damn sexy in that loose hoodie and that dark wash pair of jeans clinging to her plump ass and thick thighs. My cock was loving it. Though I knew this level of sexual tension was unsustainable in the long term, the thought of toying with her won over. So, I marched to the office with her and texted mom to tell her that I didn't want to change rooms.

My parents rarely show interest in me other than what I can contribute to the family. I've been bred to be the perfect Livingston heir since birth, my path drilled into me. The only reason I go to Heathcliff is so that I can get into a prestigious university and continue the family name. My parents don't keep tabs on my spending or who I sleep with and in return, I follow their life plan. It's a convenient arrangement, though disappointing.

"Isn't that shirt too tight for you, cupcake?" I catch one of the boys standing around Katie pointing to her. Henry. He's a new student too, but he's made friends with all the wrong boys. He's always making fun of Katie's beautiful body and though it makes me angry, I can't say anything in public without appearing to be besotted with her. "Looks like you're going to have to cut down on the cupcakes you eat at the cafeteria."

A few of them laugh behind her back and I notice Katie's eyes shutter. Her lips press together in a tight line. She wants to say something, but she doesn't.

At the end of my patience, I stand up, stalking my prey. "Hey, didn't I tell you to stay away from my toy?" I drop my ass in the empty seat next to Katie's and put my arm around her shoulder like she's my property. I love touching her because it's the only way I get to feel that soft body against mine. Katie's blue eyes turn to me, sharp and filled with fire.

The Bully's Milky Roommate

I love it when she looks at me like that like I'm the only one who can get under her skin.

"Math, huh. That one isn't due until the end of the week. Do you ever have fun, cupcake?" I glance at the homework she's working on. Henry leaves her alone, returning to his seat, now that I'm here to torment her. When my hand slips lower, I brush the side of her breast. Instantly, Katie moans, the sound making my cock twitch in response.

Instantly, my mind is transported to last evening, the way I pushed her against the wall and ground into her little pussy. My attraction to her burns through my body. I'd barely worked off my sexual frustration during practice last evening. But then, I came to find a picture of that sexy dress Katie had designed. I was surprised to know that she wanted to be a fashion designer. I always thought she wanted to get a degree, from the way she keeps studying. I hoarded that little secret deep in my mind as I let her ride my cock needily. When she closed her eyes, I wanted to kiss her so bad. But then, sense dawned on me.

I jacked off to images of her in that dress in the shower, hoping she didn't hear me. She has no idea how much she affects me.

"Are you thinking about how you rode me shamelessly last night? I quite liked the dress you made." I whisper in her ear, teasing her. Katie's eyes widen as she turns to me. "Don't act so scared, no one knows your secret yet."

Have her tits gotten bigger or were they already that huge? I turn to her chest which is covered by the blazer and it does look like she's gained a bit of weight. It makes me want to peel that shirt away and paw at those ripe, plump breasts.

"You're not gonna tell anyone, are you?" She appears

mortified at the thought of people knowing she makes clothes. I don't know why she's so scared, since I think it's pretty admirable that she has a dream.

"That depends."

"On?"

"What can you give me?" I ask her. "What will you give me if I keep your secret?"

"Anything." Her voice is desperate. "Just please...don't tell anyone. My parents don't know yet and I don't want it getting back to them."

Anything. The offer is tempting. "Why not?"

"They want me to go to college," Katie says, her eyes still conflicted. "I...I wanted to achieve something concrete before I tell them." She pauses and realizes she's said too much. "Anyway, I'll give you whatever you want. Just name your price."

"What if I ask for more than you can give?" My eyes bore into hers and her eyelashes drop when she realizes what I'm hinting at. "Sex, baby. Can you give me that?"

I'm just playing with her. No matter how bad I wanted to sleep with her, I wouldn't force her into it. I just want to scare her and see how her expression changes. As predicted, her eyes grow bigger. She swallows and I tamp down the urge to kiss her full lips. "You want....to sleep with me?"

"You think you can do that, cupcake?" My hands squeeze her shoulders as she struggles to take a breath. "You think you can let your bully fuck you and scream his name when you come?"

A flicker of heat passes through her sapphire irises before it's forgotten. "Bryan....."

The teacher walks in and I back off, my body on fire. "Forget it," I tell her. "I was kidding. I'll come up with a suitable punishment for you."

The Bully's Milky Roommate

Standing up, I stalk to the front, my heart thudding the entire time. I thought being roommates with Katie would be easy, but between my attraction to her and the wealth of secrets she's hiding, it's becoming an exercise in self-control. I can't cross the line. I can't let her find out how attracted I am to her. But god, the thought of fucking that curvy, soft body keeps me hard for the rest of the class.

* * *

I'm hungry when I come back to my room after school. Technically, I was supposed to be at practice, but I came back to grab a new shirt and my shoes. I walk around the empty room, gazing at Katie's open laptop. It's in screen-saver mode. Her bed is empty and she hasn't been sewing. Isn't she back yet?

Grabbing my water bottle, I push the bathroom door open, reach for the basin, and freeze.

"Bryan." Katie stands up from where she was sitting, her eyes big as saucers. My gaze trails lower and my jaw drops to the floor. The dull sound of a pump whirring is the only thing I can hear for the next few seconds. Heat courses through my body at the sight of Katie half-naked in the bathroom, a breast pump attached to her massive tits. My cock goes hard as steel in my pants. Two bottles are attached to her pump and they're rapidly filling up with white milk as I stand there, still as a grave.

Panicked, Katie turns off the breast pump, but she doesn't pull it off her breasts. Because that would mean I could see her bare tits. Her milk-filled bare tits.

"What the fuck—" My eyes sting with lust at the sight of my curvy roommate standing naked from the waist up, pumping her breasts in our en-suite bathroom. The scent of sweet, nutty milk coats the air, making me lick my lips in arousal.

None of my fantasies even come close to the real thing. Katie's curvy body is mesmerizing in its nakedness, her fat, plump breasts falling heavy over her soft waist like two watermelons. No wonder her tits felt big this morning. She's been producing milk.

I try to rack my brain for an explanation and remember from Biology class that women lactate when they're pregnant or after giving birth. Is Katie—

"I thought you had practice today." Those are the first words that spill from her lips. Maybe she wants me to get out, but I'm not going anywhere until I find out what's going on.

"I...came back to grab my bag." I'm speechless for the first time in my life, worst-case scenarios running through my head. Does Katie have a boyfriend? Did he knock her up? Is that why she's lactating at eighteen? "What the...are you pregnant, Katie?"

"No!" She stumbles forward and hits her knee on the toilet seat, losing balance. I step in to grab her as she falls onto me, her big breasts bouncing up and down as I catch her. One of my hands grabs her breast pump and accidentally pulls it off. My other hand curves around her naked waist, holding her in place. Her sore, red nipples fill my view, fat and dotted with white cream. Her tender tits jiggle, spraying cream onto my shirt. That jiggle goes straight to my groin. God, she's so damn sexy. I should be disgusted, but I'm so turned on by the sight of her full, milky tits.

We stare at each other, both refusing to move. Her chest rises and falls with every breath, my mouth growing dry. I want to lick those fat, red nipples and swallow them whole.

The Bully's Milky Roommate

God, the thought of suctioning those massive milkers with my mouth and feeling that nutty cream explodes inside my mouth is enough to make me come in my pants.

I can't stop myself from leaning forward, from burying my face between her soft, pillowy tits and taking a whiff of that sweet titty milk. God, my cock wants to come inside her so bad. I kiss and nibble her bare skin, tasting how soft she is under my hot mouth. Het tits are hypnotic, begging me to suck on them like candy.

"I'll make a deal with you." My lips trail down the curve of her breast, touching one engorged, nipple. When I kiss it, she moans loudly, her sensitive body reacting to my mouth. My tongue darts out and circles her wet, swollen teat. I lick the sweet cream coating the surface of her teat, the novel taste of titty milk driving me insane. My stomach grunts in response, wanting to fill itself with her nourishing cream. I'm hungry for more than food. I'm hungry for her and I need her so bad right now.

"Bryan..." She shudders in my arms, closing her eyes. "What are you...." She stops talking when I roll my tongue over her aroused nipple. My cock throbs in my pants, aching to bury itself inside her heat. I bet she's wet from all that pumping. God, I never would've thought Katie was hiding a secret like this.

"If you let me milk you, I won't tell anyone about your designs."

"What?" She can't focus with my mouth driving her insane.

"You said you'd do anything. I want you to let me milk you whenever I want in exchange for keeping your secret. Secrets, now that I know how sweet you taste."

I close my lips around her bare tip and suck hard. "Oh my god..." She shakes in my arms as her letdown hits. Milk floods into my mouth and I swallow it all down like a starving beast. It tastes so good and warm as it slides down my throat, opening me up to the forbidden taste of my milky roommate. She's everything I've wanted and more. I suction her tit harder, letting her slip her fingers into my hair. "Yes... oh my god...more...your mouth feels so good."

I lick and nibble at her squishy tip, pulling on it to draw out more of her precious, sweet liquid. The more I drink, the more addicted I become. I want to touch her tits, to squeeze and play with them while I milk her. When the milk supply trickles to drops, I pop her tip out, kissing her sore nipple.

"I need you on a bed, cupcake." I bend down and lift her up, carrying her out in my arms.

"Bryan, I'm heavy. You don't have to carry me—" Katie's eyes burst open, her fist resting against my chest. "Put me down."

"Did you forget I play football? I could carry two of you, Katie." I carry her to her bed and lay her down before climbing on top of her. It's only now that I notice she's still wearing her school uniform skirt. "Take off your skirt."

"What?" Katie blinks.

"You heard me, cupcake. I want you naked while I milk you." My gaze is on her bare tits, hot and hungry. God, she looks so beautiful laid out under me, her tits on display. Milk coats her full nipple, making her appear so tempting. I can see the soft folds of her stomach that disappear into her skirt. I want to see her in her entirety. "If we're going to do this, I need to see you. All of you."

There's a flicker of hesitation in her eyes. She doesn't move. Instead, I feel her walls coming down as she closes in on herself.

"I..." She turns her face away. "I'm not comfortable with my body. Can we close the curtains?"

My heart breaks at the sight of her hesitation. It hurts even more to know I made her doubt herself.

"No. I want to see your body in the daylight. Every single inch of it." I grab her chin and make her look at me. Her lips are trembling. "Is this about what the guys at school said today?" When she remains silent, I go on, "I don't care about your weight, Katie. I just want to feel your skin against mine when I milk you." I lower my lips, ghosting her ears. "And I know you're soaked between your legs right now, so let me make it better for you, okay?"

Katie's sharp intake of breath tells me all I need to know. When I reach for the zipper of her skirt, she doesn't stop me. I pull it down and slip the piece of fabric off her body, throwing it onto the floor. Her soft, thick thighs fill my vision, making me catch my breath. My cock pulses against her thigh, wanting to spread those legs apart and bury itself in her heat. God, she is the picture of fertile, feminine beauty with those wide hips, soft stomach, and big thighs. Her white panties cling to her soaked pussy, the wet patch visible right up to her mound.

She breaths evenly, looking at me like my validation could make or break her. Against my self-preservation instinct, I give her the truth. "God, you're so sexy. All soft curves and creamy skin." I slide a palm down her curvy hips, making goosebumps break out all over her skin. Her bare nipples bead, aching for my touch. I brush my thumb against her hip, dipping my head to kiss her stomach. Her core pulls in, startled by my gesture. "Someday, I'm going to kiss every inch of this body and eat that pussy leisurely. But today, I need to feel you come around my fingers when I milk you. Do you think you can do that for me, baby?" I try to keep my voice gentle so that I don't startle her.

"Bryan..." Katie's voice is wispy.

"Open those legs for me, Katie." I push one hand between her legs and she obeys.

Katie opens her legs for me, torn between trust and fear. I remind myself that I'm just her bully and it's not my job to restore her faith in men, but damn, if I don't want to slay her demons and make her smile. She's always been my weakness. The fact that we're roommates is just making my affliction worse.

I cup her mound and she whines breathily as I tease the damp patch of fabric covering her pussy lips. "So fucking wet." I run a digit up and down her covered seam, making milk bubble from her tips. "Does milking make you horny?"

"Yes." She closes her eyes and throws her head back, letting me play with her pussy. My petting calms her down and I let her breathe easy as I feel her pussy under my fingers.

"You're dying to get off, aren't you?" I use my other hand to cup her full breast, gently massaging her aching mound. When she begins leaking more cream, I lower my head to her nipple and lick it all off. Pushing away the fabric at her crotch, I touch her bare, wet folds. The feel of her uncovered pussy, those glistening pink folds quivering, goes straight to my groin. I grind my bulge against her thigh, groaning. "There, does that feel better?"

"Yeah..." Her fingers slide into my hair, pulling me closer to her breast. When my thumb teases her hard little clit, she arches her back, pushing her aroused teat between my lips. I swallow down her bare nipple and suck on it. Instantly, her pussy reacts, clenching as I drink a mouthful of her milk. It's not enough. I don't think it ever will be.

The Bully's Milky Roommate

Continuing to tease and rub her little pearl with my thumb, I slide my middle finger up her folds, finding her leaking cunt. I slip it into her hole, feeling how her fingers clench in my hair. "Bryan...oh god..." She's breathless with pleasure as I push my finger deeper into her empty cunt, feeling her fleshy walls coat me in juices.

My mouth pulls and drinks from her teat, milking her on the bed as I play with her bare pussy. Her pussy is so tight that it can't even fit another finger, making me wonder if she's a virgin. When I suckle on her bud again, she clenches around me. That gets me moving. I begin thrusting my middle finger in and out of her hot sex, feeling how she responds to the friction hungrily. Katie drips all over my finger, wet and ready. I push another finger inside her, taking care of her tender flesh. The milking has her horny as hell, because she takes it easily, calling out my name as I drink from her bare tits.

Two fingers move inside her channel as milk floods my mouth. Her body goes all tight and hot as I finger fuck her on her bed, drinking down her moans. Her sweetness is a drug that I need to survive, her heat closing around me.

"Bryan....I...I'm coming." Her voice is the last thing I hear before she spasms around my fingers. "Bryan!" Katie comes with a scream, calling out my name as she climaxes against my knuckle, her body soft and pliant. I suckle on her nipple, one hand squeezing her tit for every last drop of cream. My roommate climaxes, her pleasure traveling through me. My cock is roaring in my pants, aching to come with her, but I can't lose control like that. I can't let her see how much she affects me.

When I stop suckling on her sweet nipple, she's still spasming around my fingers. I raise my head, licking the cream off my lips and staring into Katie's flushed face. I continue fucking her pussy with my fingers until her contractions slow down moments later. Katie's big, blue eyes crack open, looking so vulnerable and beautiful in the afternoon light. I want to kiss those pink lips and tell her how bad I want her, but I pull my fingers out before I can do anything so stupid.

With one final kiss to her breasts, I stumble off the bed, her juices still coating my fingers. Katie stares at me, slightly recovering from the aftershocks of her orgasm.

I'm shaken from the inside out, the sight of her naked body affecting me deeply. I stare at her lying there for a second before reaching out for my bag. She waits for me to say something but I play the part of the asshole. I want to make her feel used, not like she's upended my entire world.

Turning my back to her, I reach for the door.

"I'll see you at night."

With that, I leave the room, closing it behind me. My heart aches for leaving her alone and my legs want to drag me back there to tell her how well she did. Part of me wants to lavish her with praises, kiss, and hold her after that milking session, but it's out of the question. Milking is her punishment, not her pleasure.

I stumble down the hallway and find a men's room that's empty. I shut myself in a stall and drop my pants. My cock is leaking pre-cum, erect, and aching for release. Feeling Katie come on my fingers, her bare tits in my mouth was the best kind of fantasy. I wanted to finish inside her, but I can't cross that line yet. I wrap my slick-coated fingers around my dick, smearing her release all over my throbbing shaft. Then, I fist myself, sliding up and down. I close my eyes and picture her naked body, those fat tits out on display, her soft thighs open and welcoming, and her fertile hips tempting me into spilling. I come hard and fast in a few strokes, spurting all over the tiled wall. My climax seizes my veins, giving me the relief I've wanted ever since I saw her pumping in our bathroom.

It takes me a few moments after coming to catch my breath. I reach for the toilet paper to wipe off my dick and the walls so that nobody finds out about my secret addiction to my roommate. Once I'm clean and dry, I zip my pants up and grab my bag. I still need to make it to practice, though I doubt I'm going to be able to focus with the image of Katie's naked body burned into my mind. She'll be all I think of for a while.

God, what induced me to milk her? Just one sight of those fleshy, milky tits and I was attacking her like a hungry beast. Nobody can make me lose it like her.

I look down at my phone which is flooded with texts from my teammates asking me where I am. I mutter a curse under my breath and reply to them.

Bryan: On my way.

Chapter 3
Katie

"Hey, Katie." Saumya catches me on my way to class the next day, a list in her hand. Instantly, I come to a stop, remembering my request to get my roommate changed. She comes to stand before me, dressed in a navy suit. "I wanted to talk to you about the room situation."

I pause on one side of the path, blinking at Saumya. It's weird that I haven't thought about getting away from Bryan since last evening. My cheeks heat as my mind floods with images of my bully roommate milking me on my bed last night. It was the most exciting, erotic thing in my life. When he put his mouth to my nipples and sucked, I was transported to heaven. It was everything I'd been longing for, but it all came crashing down when Bryan left me abruptly after I embarrassingly orgasmed on his fingers.

As I lay on that bed, naked and sated, Bryan's spit coating my drained nipples, I felt used. He'd been so gentle with me, so nice to me when he milked me. He said he didn't care about my weight and for one moment, I felt like I was at the top of the world. Every lick of his tongue on my breast was pure pleasure. When he pushed his finger into my pussy and stretched me, I wanted to come right away. It's like Bryan knows all my sweet spots. He played me like a violin and I totally fell for his act. I'm so stupid to be attracted to him. He only milked me because of our deal—his silence in exchange for my milk.

"I'm sorry we can't do anything about it right now. I know it must be uncomfortable for you to live with a guy, but I promise I'll move Bryan as soon as Josh graduates."

Josh? Who is Josh? I've been woolgathering.

"When will Josh graduate?" I ask, hoping she hasn't gone through that before.

"In three months. That's the earliest I can get Bryan a new room."

I'm surprised Bryan can't find his own room, especially because his family practically owns the school. Surely, they can pull some strings to get him his own private room.

"That's fine," I utter distractedly, wondering if I should take this up with Bryan directly. My cheeks heat at the thought of him gazing at me with those moss-green eyes that make my core burn. Now that he's discovered my milky secret, I don't think he's going to leave. Not until our deal is done. "I can wait for three months."

"Really?" Saumya's dark brown eyes light up. "That's great. I thought you'd be disappointed. You were so keen on moving out."

"Uh...I guess I've had time to adjust to my new situation." Bryan and I aren't friends, not by a long shot, but we've come to a sort of understanding. One that involves him making me come naked and draining my tits. I know it's wrong and I know he's only using me, but I can't help but want more. Only when we're carrying out our deal am I allowed to indulge my forbidden attraction for my bully.

"That's great. Bryan says you guys are getting along well, which is more than I hoped for. Let me know if you have any problems, okay?"

I nod my head and Saumya marches away, more upbeat. Bryan told her we're getting along? When? I didn't see him last night before I slept. However, his bed appeared crumpled when I woke up this morning. He must've crept in late at night and gone to class early. It's disappointing, but it gives me some time to process my feelings.

I walk slowly to class, my mind receiving a jolt the moment my eyes land on Bryan. The hit of his vivid green irises is like a splash of cold water. I can't read his expression at all, but my body begins to grow warm, nevertheless. I pumped before class, but when I pushed my finger between my legs, I wished it were his finger inside me, making me feel as good as yesterday. I wished for his hot, soft lips on my tits instead of the mechanical pump, suctioning me just the way I like. He's sitting far away from me like he's trying to avoid me. Usually, he'd stand up and give me a snide remark, but today, he's busy chatting with his teammates.

"Hey, fatso, had a good night's sleep?" One of his teammates taunts me. Just the usual. I roll my eyes, pretending to be unaffected. I'm immune to their petty taunts now, or that's what I saw myself.

"Leave her alone." My jaw literally drops at his words. Is he defending me? Talk about mixed signals. His teammates, who share my shock, turn to him with narrowed eyes. "I'm not in the mood to play with Katie, not when our team could be losing against our rival."

That gets their minds screwed on straight. "You're right, we need a strategy for the upcoming tournament."

They ignore me and move to discussing football strategies. I've never been to Bryan's games, but I hear the rumors

The Bully's Milky Roommate

around school and I know an important tournament is coming up. Maybe that's why he's been practicing so hard. I move all the way to the back of the classroom and occupy my usual seat. However, when I take out my books and look up, Bryan is gazing at me.

* * *

I stifle a yawn, stretching my hands outside the library. It's almost dark, and the streetlights are beginning to come on. After class, I pumped in my room and spent the whole afternoon studying in the library. I walk out of the red-brick, colonial building that creates a nostalgic atmosphere. I watch the organ twilight bounce off the cobblestone paths, disappearing behind the green trees and plants. Heathcliff Academy consists of several historical buildings dating back to the colonial era. Walking through the campus makes me feel like I've gone back in time. I pass by the main building which looks like the white house with its long pillars and rectangular body. I'm so glad I get to go here. Despite Bryan's bullying and my unfriendly classmates, I have fallen in love with Heathcliff Academy. I can't believe I just have one more year to go before I graduate.

My tits ache a little, already filling up, as I pass by the large football field. They're always sore these days. I linger there for a moment, watching the players walk away after practice. Doesn't Bryan play football too? My eyes scan the field for my roommate and chance upon my bully. His green gaze meets me and I'm stuck in place, unable to escape. Bryan stares at me, waiting for his teammates to disappear. Then, he jogs up to me, his scent filling my nostrils. I clutch my bag close to my hip, letting him give me a once-over. My traitorous nipples tighten when his gaze rakes over my chest. I'm still wearing my school uniform, but I ache to be milked by him. It felt so good to have his mouth suckling on my breasts and his thick fingers moving inside me last night. I don't think I can ever go back to my sterile, mechanical pump after that.

"Hey." He says, surveying the empty space behind me. Lots of students are returning to the dorm and it's not unusual to see Bryan bullying me. As if aware of their gazes, he raises his hand and places it on the side of the wire net, caging me home. "Going back to the dorm?"

"Yeah. I was at the library all day, studying." I don't know why I'm telling him that.

"Wait for me. I'll get showered and join you."

"Ummm...it's okay...I really need to get home." His eyes flicker to my growing tits and he knows what I need. My heart thumps louder, making my need known. Damn, I wish I wasn't so weak, so needy for my bully roommate's touch.

Bryan drops his voice. "Cupcake, you either wait or I drag you into the shower with me and we can do it together." His mouth touches my earlobe and pleasure snakes down the back of my neck. I'll never admit this out loud but I love when he talks dirty to me. "Besides, it's been more than twenty-four hours since I milked you. According to our deal, I get to suck on those titties once a day."

I blush like a beet at the mention of my titties. The earthy scent of his sweat makes me want to beg him to drain my titties. My teats are sore and needy for Bryan's mouth.

"When did we ever come up with that deal?" I ask, looking around to make sure nobody can hear us. My fingertips brush his and sparks flood my system. God, I'm really horny for him.

"Last night. I get to drink from you whenever I want in

exchange for keeping your secret, remember?" He's so cute when he gives me that lopsided boyish smile. If he weren't my bully, I'd totally fall for him. "I know two of your secrets now so maybe I should change the deal to milking you a minimum of two times a day."

"You like milking me that much?" The words were supposed to sound sarcastic, but they sound needy.

"Yeah." He admits after a long pause, his fingers brushing my soft blonde hair. "I like milking you a lot. Those fat titties are every man's fantasy."

His complimentary words take me by surprise. He's usually nasty to me but his words make me warm. "I didn't know you were a tits guy." I've never been so bold before but I can't take the words back once they're out.

"Me neither," Bryan confesses, his fingers brushing the lower curve of my breast. I moan, feeling sensitive to his touch. God, what's happening to me? "You're delicious, Katie."

His breathy words betray a lack of control he's never exhibited before. When he spies his teammate coming toward us, he backs away.

"Hey." He smiles at him on his way to the showers, leaving my body feeling all kinds of hot. But I don't miss the way he watches over me, making sure his friends don't bully me while I'm waiting for him. Could he be protecting me?

I watch Bryan's broad back disappear, shaking my head. He'd been bullying me all this time. Why would be try to protect me? However, once the idea takes root, weird facts begin to align. Bryan doesn't let anyone else talk down to me. He's never called me fat or chubby, just 'cupcake'. He shuts the other guys down when they try to toy with me. Could I have been mistaken about his intentions all along?

My mind churns and churns while I sit on a bench at

the edge of the grass, waiting for Bryan to finish showering. The tips of his hair are still wet, his body smelling of deodorant and an aqua body wash when he finally re-appears. He's wearing one of those tight, form-hugging t-shirts that cling to his biceps and pecs, revealing his delicious body. His shorts cover his taut ass, his tall shadow blanketing me. God, he's so hot and sexy with those green eyes and jock physique. If it weren't for his weird milky bog boobs addiction, he wouldn't even look twice at me.

"You waited." He remarks his lopsided grin lighting sparks in my heart.

"You left me no choice." I stand up, walking next to Bryan as the sun sinks lower into the horizon. "You've been extra busy these days."

"Yeah, the first championship of the season is coming up." Bryan swings his backpack over one shoulder, keeping a healthy distance from me. "I want the team to start on the right note with a win. We've all been practicing extra hard." He turns to me. "Actually, the first match is going to be here at Heathcliff. Why don't you come?"

"You're inviting me to your football match?" My eyes widen, surprised. "Is this some twisted sort of power play?"

He smiles and for the first time, I feel a sense of kinship to him. We walk side-by-side, like we're friends and it makes me long for more with him. "Isn't everyone at Heathcliff interested in the team?"

"I don't know the first thing about football," I admit.

"You could learn," he says, keeping his tone light. This new, friendly side of Bryan is confusing me. Has becoming roommates and his personal milking toy changed our dynamic somehow? I'm too afraid to hope. "Come to the game and find out how exciting football can be."

We walk another few steps until the dorm appears in the distance.

"You wanna play football professionally?" I ask. "I mean, you're the team captain and you practice pretty religiously."

"Hell no. I'm just doing it to make my dad happy. He was part of the football team at Heathcliff too." Bryan tucks his big hands into his pockets and I inhale unevenly.

"Really?" I had no idea Bryan's parents went here. "It must be nice following your family's legacy. I wish I could "

He blinks at me. "Cupcake, I don't usually say this to people but trust me when I say I wish I had a passion like you."

"You mean like fashion?"

"Yeah. It's cool. I don't know why you want to keep it a secret." He swallows. "I mean, it's good for me since I get to suck on your tits whenever I like." I blush. "You like it when I say that."

"I...don't."

"It turns you on. You blush every time I mention your tits."

"That's because it's...naughty. Roommates aren't supposed to mention tits." I turn to him. "Especially male roommates."

"You already know we're more than roommates." His voice is like sandpaper, filled with lust and longing.

"Don't," I say, holding myself back. My feet stop moving next to a tree that overlooks the dorm. The streetlights have come on, illuminating Bryan's dreamboat looks. "I know you're only doing this for revenge. My body...I know I'm not your type." I meet his eyes, trying to hide the feeling of rejection. "Trust me, after the way you abandoned me in bed yesterday, I don't expect sweet talk from you. I...get what we're doing."

"Do you?" Bryan's voice drops to a lethal tone. If I didn't know better, I'd think he sounded angry. He takes a step forward, crowding my space until I'm walking backward. My spine hits the tree trunk, shrouding us both in shadows. Bryan's hand reaches out and he cages me, lowering his face so that his eyes are staring into mine. I drop my books in panic, biting down on my lower lip. I can't back down, not when he's trying to intimidate me.

"Yeah, you've been making fun of me for being fat all year. You bully me for my body type, Bryan. Isn't that why you find my fashion design amusing? You think I'm a joke for trying to create a fashion line for plus-sized women."

He raises his eyebrows, not moving. "You want to create a fashion line for plus-size women? That's your dream."

I swallow, remaining silent. When I avert my gaze, Bryan says, "I never made fun of you for being fat."

"Oh yeah, why do you call me cupcake, then?" My eyes flash with fire.

"Because you're sweet enough to eat." The way his growly voice says those words makes heat flood my sore.

"I don't believe you. You've been calling me cupcake because I eat too many of them and have been gaining weight."

"I don't care if you gain weight," Bryan says, his hands sliding lower. I emit an involuntary moan when his fingers sink into my hips, squeezing. "I love holding these lush curves, Katie. You have no idea how wild they drive me." His lips are hot when they touch my ear, sliding down the curve of my cheek.

"Bryan, what are you doing?" I'm breathless with need, panting in his arms as he pushes his hand up my skirt, fondling my big thighs. My hands unconsciously curve around him, feeling his back muscles flex as he moves his hand higher.

"I hate how you hide behind those oversized clothes. Do you know how hard your curves make me? Is that why you're hiding them for me?" His fingers cup my thigh, stroking the inside of my thigh with his thumb. Heat shoots up my core, and my milky tits are feeling heavy all of a sudden. "I dream of fucking that tight pussy every night, of getting to see your naked, curvy body laid out under me while I drive into you and watch those big tits bounce. Every inch of fat on your skin is precious to me, cupcake."

His words are everything I've ever wanted to hear. But they don't make sense.

"You ran away after seeing me last night," I accuse, needing his touch more than I need my next breath. "You were disgusted by me. Isn't that why you let the boys talk shit about my body?"

He pauses, guilt warring with desire for a moment.

"I was losing control," he admits. "The moment I saw your naked body, I wanted to blow all over your milky tits. Baby, do you have any idea how many times I've fantasized about fucking those massive tits? Just the thought of you in that blue dress, waiting for me to take it off you, was enough to make me come in the shower."

"You jacked off to...me?" It's unbelievable.

"You turn me into a beast, cupcake. Your body is the only one I want. I know I shouldn't have let the boys criticize your beautiful curves, but I wanted to protect you by bullying you myself."

"Wait a minute." His logic is twisted, but somehow, I get it. I reach for Bryan's jaw, cupping it and pushing his face away from mine to gaze into his eyes. "You were...

protecting me? That's bullshit. Ever since I started at Heathcliff, you've bullied me. I don't even know what I did to piss you off, but you've made me your toy."

"You rejected me first," he says, dead serious.

"What?" I blink, my mind blank.

"The day you started at Heathcliff. I asked you out and you rejected me." I try to jog my memory and suddenly, it hits me. I barely remember the first time Bryan spoke to me. I was distracted and feeling nervous about being in a new school, so I rejected his offer.

"Oh my god." Realization tumbles into my head.

"You were everything I wanted. Your curvy body had me in a chokehold the moment I lay eyes on you. But you broke my heart, cupcake. I didn't know how else to process the pain except bully you. I guess in my mind, I was protecting you from the other guys."

"You were..." I can't believe what I'm hearing. Bryan has had feelings for me for months and all this time, I thought that he was bullying me. He was saving me for himself instead. "You had no right to. I could've made friends... gotten to know other people if you hadn't singled me out."

His breath is uneven and I know I've crossed a line. Bryan might've confessed to being attracted to me, but he's still twice my size and powerful. The past doesn't change the power dynamic we have now. A long, pregnant pause passes. Bryan's hand falls away and I regret confronting him. My body needs him and now that I know he's got feelings for me, I want him even more.

"I'm sorry," he says in a low voice, making me realize that I'm still holding his jaw. "I guess I was immature and possessive. I wanted you so bad that I didn't care how I got you."

Possessive.

The Bully's Milky Roommate

No guy has ever been possessive over me. Though I'm annoyed, it also turns me on to be desired by him. The thought of Bryan Livingston wanting me, being obsessed with me, and being possessive of me ticks all my fantasies. God, I never thought I'd ever feel that way, but the truth has brought down the walls between us. Though I don't know if I can forgive him, I know it wasn't easy for him to tell me the truth.

When his dark green gaze meets mine, my defenses melt away. My heart doesn't care about what he did. All that matters is he's attracted to me, to my curvy body and lush curves. All my life, I've been criticized for the way I look, but in Bryan's eyes, I see the desire that I need to heal. I want to be wanted by someone the way he wants me. Regardless of his intentions, his feelings are genuine. I had no idea Bryan was hiding a broken heart under all that bravado.

"What are you going to do about it?" My voice is breathy but challenging.

He blinks. "Do you want me to stop with the deal?" he asks. "Leave you alone and keep my mouth shut?

"No." I don't want that at all. I don't want him to become distant again. I want him to come closer.

"Then tell me what you want, baby." His raspy voice ignites my nerves.

Him. I want him.

"Kiss me." My voice is hoarse and needy.

"You wanna kiss and make up?" He quirks an eyebrow. When I don't say anything, he nods, the desire bright in his eyes. "All right, cupcake."

He snakes one arm around my waist and pulls me close.

And then, his lips are on mine.

I whimper as his hot mouth finds mine, sealing us in a searing kiss. My toes curl, my lips responding to his hard mouth with eagerness. Heat trickles down my spine as he nibbles and explores the contours of my mouth, sucking on my lower lip like it's a juicy peach.

"Mmm...you taste so good, baby." His voice makes me feel like I'm flying like there's just the two of us in the world.

Bryan kisses me harder and I can't resist holding him, feeling his hard body flex against mine. He pulls me close, smashing our mouths together again, drinking me in like I'm the water he needs to live. My tits flatten against his chest, leaking milk onto my shirt. I don't even care because all I feel is Bryan's mouth on me.

It's my first kiss and it's transcendent. Every cell in my body sparks to life, magnetized to Bray's presence. His tongue teases the seam of my lips. When I open my mouth, he drives it in, licking and tasting my tongue. His flavor seeps through my tissues, the awareness of him in my arms engulfing me. His hands roam over my body, aching to touch my skin, but settling for cupping my tits through fabric. When he gently squeezes one heavy mound, French kissing me outside the dorm, I cry out into his mouth, needing more.

I feel his bulge rub against my stomach and I know he's aroused. We both need this so bad.

"Take me to our room," I tell him, breaking the kiss.

"What are we going to do when we get there, cupcake?" His words are tentative, yet knowing. He knows what I want, what both our bodies need.

"I want you to fuck me, Bryan Livingston."

Chapter 4
Bryan

Katie and I burst into our room, hands all over each other. I push her blazer away, kicking the door shut and bolting it. Her hands caress my bare chest as she pulls my t-shirt off. I raise my hands, helping her get it off just as her skirt falls to the floor. Our lips are fused together, the kiss steaming up our room. I pull her shirt off, leaving her in just her bra and panties. My pants come off too, my briefs molded around my thickening erection.

"Bryan..." Katie is breathless as I break the kiss, gazing into her bright blue eyes. I pull the scrunchie off her ponytail and watch as her silky blonde hair falls like a waterfall over her shoulders.

"Baby, you're breathtaking." I rasp, kissing her swollen lips again. "God, I can't believe you want me."

I push Katie onto the bed, letting her lie down before I climb over her. My eyes trace her beautiful, lush body, committing each curve to memory. Watching her milky breasts rise and fall under her red bra that cups her fat mounds is hypnotic. I want to pull it away and feast on her bare, juicy tits. Katie's fingers slide lower, gently palming my hard cock through my underwear.

"I am dying to see those fat titties naked, cupcake." I groan when she pushes her hand into my briefs, stroking my leaking head with her soft fingers. My cock is hard as steel, the grade of her fingers on my sensitive head making me leak pre-cum. Lowering my head, I kiss her plump tits that are spilling out of her red bra. Her bra is soaked, the scent of milk drugging me.

"Bryan…" she moans, trying to rub her pussy against my erection. "You're so big and thick. I love feeling your cock."

"Mmmm…baby, you touching me makes me so hard. You feel so good in my arms, baby. I love how curvy and soft your body is." I run my lips over her soft skin, squeezing and feeling every inch of her body with my hands. Katie pushes my briefs down as I grab her panties, tearing them off her sexy mound. When I run my fingers over her slick, swollen folds, she moans and arches her back. "Feeling good, baby?"

"Yeah…" The way her big blue eyes gaze at me, filled with desire and longing, is my undoing. Her thumb circles my tip and I groan, unable to stop myself. My hands unclasp her bra and tear it away from those massive milkers. My cock goes rock-hard the moment I am hit with the beauty of her bare tits. My roommate is spread out before me, her milk jugs on full display. White milk leaks from her fat, swollen teats, making me so damn hungry.

"God, you're a vision, cupcake. I didn't say this last time but I've been coming to the sight of your curvy body in the shower ever since I saw you naked." Lowering my head, I lick one aroused teat, feeling her pussy gush in response to my mouth. The sight of her is making me hard because when she begins stroking me, a blob of pre-cum falls from my cock onto her belly. Her soft fingers trace my

The Bully's Milky Roommate

pulsing veins, making me so damn needy for that little pussy.

I rub my desire all over her soft stomach, aching to put a baby inside her already. I know we're too young to have kids and I know it's forbidden, but the thought of knocking Katie up and watching her belly swell with my baby makes me so hot.

"Bryan..." Her fingers stroke the length of my bare pole, her fingers feeling so good against my velvety skin. I'm so hard right now that I can't think. "What are you thinking?"

"I'm thinking how good you'd look with my baby inside your belly," I tell her, no longer capable of holding myself back. My lips trail over her sensitive teats, nibbling and licking her cream. "I can't wait to make you a big, milky mommy bursting with cream. I love your curvy body so much, cupcake, that I want to add curves to you. When your belly is all big and bloated, I'll make love to you every night, fucking you wherever and however I please."

Images of Katie and me living together in our own house fill my mind. I can picture her as my wife, her belly swollen with our kids. It feels so easy to imagine a life with her.

"Oh god..." Katie is so hot for my words. Her eyes flash dark at me and I know my cupcake is turned on by the thought of me breeding her.

"Do you want to have babies, Katie?" I ask her. My mouth closes around her nipple, feeling her pussy cream as I drag my fingers over it. My girl loves being milked.

"Yes," she says. "I want to be a mom someday." Her eyes open and I gaze at her beautiful, round face from between her fat tits. "I...I'd very much like to have your babies, Bryan Livingston."

There is nothing that can stop me from sucking on those

juicy tits then. My mouth latches onto one fat breast, my hands cupping and kneading her bare mound to get the milk flowing. I slurp from her juicy nipples, the taste of her forbidden cream making my cock hard as a steel pole. My fingers find her clit and tease it, feeling desire gush from her hole. She's needy and ready to take my cock.

"Oh god, Bryan...I've been aching to feel your mouth on my tits since last night." She lets go of my cock, letting my man meat rest against her thigh. With every rub of her thick thighs against my rod, desire mounts in my groin until I'm burning to bury my rod in her wet heat.

"Open your legs, baby. I need to feel that pussy wrap around my dick right now." I release her sensitive teat with a wet plop, nudging my long rod between her thighs. Pre-cum drips from my swollen head onto her engorged folds, lubricating her for our time together.

"Have you done this before, baby?" I ask her, keeping my voice gentle. I love the thought of being the first man to stretch that fat little pussy. If I have something to say about it, I'll be the last too.

"No." She whispers, doubt suddenly filling her eyes. "Is that...a problem?"

"No." I kiss her lips, reassuring her. "It makes me feel so good to know I'll be your first." I grip her tits possessively and she moans as milk drips from her swollen tips. I soothe her sore tips with my fingers as I touch her like I own her. Possessiveness courses through my blood. I know there's no going back from this. Once I make her mine, I'll want her every night. "I've been waiting for a girl like you all my life."

"You...you're—" She's shocked. "I never thought..."

"Believe it or not, I wanted my first time to be with a girl I actually care about." She blushes, realizing that it's her I care about. I press a cute kiss to her open mouth. "I won't go easy on you, cupcake. You've been driving me mad with that sexy, curvy body of yours all year." She blushes. Sensations grip my groin as the slick, sensitive head of my cock slides over her creamed folds. "I wanna breed you so bad, Katie. But I don't think we're ready to have a kid yet. Are you on birth control?"

"Yeah." She nods. "I got on birth control pills because of my lactation problem."

"Good, because I don't want anything between us when I fuck you for the first time, cupcake. I want the feel of my dick scraping your pussy to be imprinted in your mind."

"I love it when you talk dirty, Bryan. I want that too," she agrees, making me grin. We're perfectly matched. "I want to feel you inside me, Bryan."

Her desire is so sexy and I don't have it in me to make my curvy girl wait. So, I push my solid length into her, hearing her scream as I tear down her walls. Her cherry pops, raining blood over my swollen, veined dick.

"Bryan." Katie's fingers are digging into my flesh, holding onto me for comfort.

"I'm here, baby." I kiss her closed eyes, knowing that I took her cherry. She's so damn tight, and though I want to go slow, the delicious squeeze of her pussy tests the limits of my self-control. I stoke her hair. "You're doing so good."

My lips trail hot kisses over her neck and titties, feeling her relax a little when I latch onto her other breast and suck out a mouthful of cream. There's so much that it spills out the corner of my lips, but I don't stop suckling on her until she feels better.

"Mmmm...that feels good." She goes soft in my arms, letting me push a little further into her. I slide into her inch by inch, taking care not to hurt her. But as her pussy wraps around me, squeezing my swollen rod, I feel an orgasm building up. I suck on her tits harder and when her fleshy inner walls squeeze me in desperation, I push the rest of the way in until my cock is buried balls deep in her cunt.

"Look at you, taking all of me like a good girl," I murmur against her breasts, lightly biting on her nipple to make milk fountain into my mouth. I drag every breath into my lungs, wanting to explode in her cunt. But I can't come before my cupcake does.

"I feel so full," Katie's eyes open and her touch softens. She gazes deep into my eyes, her heart thudding. I lick her nipple, soothing her. "God, it's good. I never knew dicks were so big. Or maybe it's just yours." When one edge of her soft lips quirks up in a smile, I feel relieved.

"You're stroking my ego, cupcake. I'm gonna take that as an invitation to ravage that virgin cunt all night."

"You're welcome to try." I love how bold and unrestricted she is in bed. I want to see this side of her more.

My body is already on the edge and only she can take the edge off. I gently rock my hips into her, warming her up. Katie bled all over my cock, and I don't want her sacrifice to be wasted. I'm going to make her see stars tonight. My trusts grow harder and deeper as my mouth drains her breast. She loves being milked and fucked simultaneously because her climax begins to build fast.

"Bryan...don't stop....please...more...." Her breathy words are the soundtrack to the most explosive sex of my life. I pull out and jam my dick into her cunt hard. White hot light engulfs my senses as Katie screams my name.

"Bryan!" Katie's fleshy walls ripple around me, sucking my dick in. Her hucow tits bounce and slap my face, but I don't stop suctioning on her bare tits. She's still so full of milk, needing to be drained and filled. I suck on her tender, squishy nipple, driving my hips harder and harder into her, my balls slapping her big, sexy ass. She arches her back and clings to me as I fuck her brutally in her bed, not caring about who hears our screams. My body exists only to please her and to be consumed by her hot little pussy. I piston deep into her cave, feeling the opening of her womb spasm as I ride her to a climax.

"I'm coming!" I faintly hear her voice just as my orgasm seizes me. A burst of milk floods my mouth and then, she's coming.

Everything clenches for a moment, ecstasy exploding in my veins. And then, I'm coming with Katie. Her pussy spasms around my dick and she squirts, covering my massive pole in her juices.

"Oh my god..." She's screaming and crying and flying all at once, and I'm right there with her. Her hands are all over my bare flesh, my fingers squeezing her hips as I let go of her used nipple. My cock explodes into ribbons of cum, drenching her fertile pussy. Fire and joy rain down on me, my body becoming one with Katie's. The feeling of breeding her takes me even higher, making my body melt into a river of unrestricted pleasure. We both come and come, clinging to each other, fucking like animals on the single dorm bed until there's nothing but joy.

When I open my eyes several moments later, everything feels changed. The soft glow of the bedside lamp illuminates Katie's sated face. I'm still buzzing from the aftershocks of that explosive orgasm and from the way she parts her lips, she is too.

"Bryan...that was amazing....oh god, now I know why everyone keeps talking about sex."

I laugh, loving how chatty and open she is after I come inside her. "I'm glad you loved the experience, baby." I kiss her. "Because I loved it so much that I already want a repeat."

"What? Already?" Her eyes widen. "What about dinner?"

We need to go to the dining hall for dinner. I was so wrapped up in her that I almost forgot. If we don't show up there, the boys will get suspicious.

"Damn, I almost forgot about dinner." Reluctantly, I pull out of Katie's sore pussy, my cock drenched in liquids and some blood. I'm still semi-hard.

"Katie, I love your body," I tell her as she sits up. My hands stroke her hip, not wanting to stop touching her. Holding her with my gaze, I kiss her temple. "And I'm sorry for making you feel like I didn't. Baby, you're so sexy and I don't want you to believe anyone who tells you that you're not."

She giggles. "Look at you, being all nice and possessive after you fucked me. I thought jocks ran away after taking their pleasure."

"Never. I'm not gonna leave you, cupcake. Not when you have me so addicted to that cunt." I kiss her cheek. "We have a deal, remember? I get your body whenever and wherever I want."

"I thought that deal only included my tits." She's teasing and I love that she's opened up to me. I was so afraid all my bullying would scar her. From this day on, I'm going to prove to her that I deserve her.

"It includes all of you." My voice is hoarse, and I realize that I want her heart too. "We're signing a new deal, sweetie. One that involves you being my exclusive property."

"You want me to be your girlfriend?" Katie's eyes widen like she never expected me to say something so ridiculous.

The Bully's Milky Roommate

But once the words are out, I realize how much I want them to be true. I want everyone to know she's mine, but I don't think I'm ready for that yet. For that past year, I've carefully crafted an image as the hot jock, bullying Katie at every turn. That's going to have to change before I make things official.

"Yeah," I admit. "I might not be able to make things official right away, but I promise, I want you, Katie. I need time to undo the damage I've done."

"I...get it." She swallows. "I...I'd like our relationship to be a secret too. At least until I figure things out."

"That works for me, cupcake." I roll off the bed, stretching my hands over my head. "Come on, you're getting in the shower with me. Though I'd love to see you walking around the dining hall dripping cum from your pussy, I'm afraid that would get us caught. Let's get you cleaned up."

She's a naked goddess when she walks to me, her hips swaying, those empty milkers jiggling, and basically that curvy body making me hot again. I bundle us both into the shower before I can give in to my impulse to take her again.

I turn on the shower, holding Katie close to me. Waters fall over us as I kiss the back of her neck.

"Mmmm...you're so soft, baby. I don't know how I resisted you for so long."

I gently soap her body, kissing her when she feels the sting of soap against her freshly fucked pussy. It's a reminder that I took her virginity, that I made her mine in every way that matters. And it's only the beginning.

Because I need this girl. She's no longer just my roommate, she's my girlfriend.

And she doesn't know but I'm starting to develop feelings for her.

Chapter 5
Katie
One month later—

I straddle Bryan's lap, my nipples hard and poking through my tank top. His tongue is in my mouth, his hardness pressing into my wet pussy that's covered by my shorts. It's just three in the afternoon but he doesn't have practice today and I skipped studying at the library so that we could spend some time together.

"Mmm...baby, you look extra delicious today. How am I supposed to keep my hands off you?" His big hands cup my ass, squeezing my round cheeks.

"You say that every time," I chide him, my fingers slipping into his hair, needy for a kiss. "You can't keep your hands off me, Bryan."

"You're just that addictive, cupcake." When I frown, he adds, "I know you don't like that name, but I want to reclaim it for you. I'm going to call you cupcake in bed, not because you're fat, but because you're sweet enough to eat. I want to eat that sweet pussy, feast on those delicious, milky nipples, and feel that tight little cunt flexing around me when I fuck you every night. You're my sweet dessert, baby, the icing on the cake."

The Bully's Milky Roommate

"You're gonna get diabetes." I blush, his words making my toes curl. I never thought Bryan would be such a romantic boyfriend. I can speak my mind when I'm with him, and I've never had that with anyone, not even my parents.

"I don't care. You're going to be my last meal, Katie."

I can't believe I get to live this life. The day after we first made love, he told the school that I wasn't a target anymore. He's been nice to me ever since, buying me coffee. It shocks the other guys who made fun of him once but since he's the captain, he shut them down. They think he's trying to clean up his bad karma before he graduates, but nobody has any idea that he's been milking and fucking me in the dark. It feels so new and forbidden.

I even attended two of his football games, with the finals coming up in a few weeks. He winked at me when he saw me and I was red as a tomato. My feelings for him have been growing every day, but I don't know if I'm ready to go official yet.

My roommate's hands slip under my tank top, grazing the underside of my tits. When he realizes that I'm not wearing a bra, his eyes flash to me. "You're not wearing a bra, cupcake?"

"I need to be milked, boyfriend." I lean forward, pressing my tits right into his big, rough palms. He obliges me, pushing his other hand up and gently massaging my other breast. It feels so good when he touches me like that right before he milks me. I think I'm addicted.

"Baby, you know that's my favorite part of the day. I dream of these milky titties all the time."

We've been in a secret relationship for a month and in that time, we've been fucking like rabbits. It's like I can't keep my hands off him. Bryan is equally ravenous, his eyes blazing with lust every time he returns home from practice. He slowly milks me and fucks me in our bed until I'm all drained and happy. He falls asleep next to me at night and we talk about the day. Bryan listens to me go on about my apprenticeship and my dreams for a plus-size couture brand and he strokes my naked skin, telling me how much he wants to invest in that dream of mine.

"When I get my trust fund, I'm going to spend it all on helping you start your own label."

"You'd be broke then. What are you going to do if my business goes under?"

"It won't. I have faith in you."

I scoffed. "You're not such a smart investor, are you? Do you know how many new businesses fail?"

"I don't care, cupcake. Seeing you happy would make the investment worth it."

When I told him I got another rejection last week, he kissed me and said, "It's their loss. They missed out on mentoring the next big thing in fashion." Then, he kissed me and said, "You're going to be great, Katie. I know it. I mean, your designs are just so beautiful. The people who are meant to love them will love them."

I've never talked to anyone about my dream before, but having Bryan by my side gives me confidence. His point of view is a nice change from my own anxious, self-defeating thoughts. We've even moved our beds together so that we can sleep together at night. Sometimes, we do homework together and he tells me about his parents and the big Livingston townhouse. He's going to inherit it someday.

"We're gonna live there when we get married. It's in New York, right where all the fashion labels are." When I blinked, he added, "Of course, we've got a house in Paris too, if you think Europe would be better for your career."

The Bully's Milky Roommate

"Stop." I giggled, my heart soaring like an eagle. "You're already dreaming of getting married and moving with me to New York?"

He put his hands around my belly and pulled me close, kissing my hair. "Mmm...Told you I wanted to have babies with you."

Every day with him is like a dream and every time he kisses me, I come out of my shell a little more. I've started talking to the girls now that he isn't bullying me anymore, but even as I get to know the others, my heart always longs for Bryan. The special connection we have makes every other relationship pale in comparison. He's always smiling at me, letting me silently know that he's got my back. And every time I look into those eyes, I find myself falling deeper in love with him.

Bryan pulls my tank top over my breasts, revealing my engorged, massive mounds. They've been growing bigger every day, thanks to his milking. At first, I wanted to get rid of the uncomfortable, achy feeling, but I've started loving it. When Bryan rolls his tongue over my tender nipple, I feel heat bloom in my core.

Just then, the phone begins to ring. Without thinking, I reach out for it. There's a New York number on the screen. Bryan raises his head, studying the number before he says, "Answer it."

"Hello?" I answer the phone, the feel of Bryan's lips on my bare titties drugging my senses. He doesn't stop licking my teats, his touches distracting me.

"This is Katrina from the House of Accardo. Am I speaking to Katie Mendelson?"

Bryan's lips circle my wet tips and when he latches on, I moan loudly into the phone. My legs wrap around him, watching his green eyes fix me with a knowing, naughty stare as he steadily sucks cream from my breast.

"I want to speak to you about the apprenticeship you applied for. Is this a good time?"

Bryan cups my heavy mounds, gently squeezing. I can't think, but I breathily reply, "Yes."

"Great. I'm happy to inform you that you've gotten into our apprenticeship program. Our founder was really impressed by your interview last week."

Bryan can hear her voice even though I'm not on speaker. He grins in that knowing way before sucking harder on my teats. Milk explodes into his mouth and flows down his hard lips, spraying on my thighs. My breath grows uneven, my pleasure spiking.

"T-thank you." I can barely think straight with my boyfriend milking me. My pussy grinds on his hard-on, needy. Just the scent, the feel, the sight of Bryan makes me so horny.

"I'll send you an e-mail with the details soon. We have a minimum grade threshold for incoming apprentices and we're having an open day this winter. It'd be great if you could make it. Many interns use it as an opportunity to get a feel for our label."

Bryan pulls his mouth off one teat and squeezes my breasts together. Then, he sinks his fingers into my plump mounds and makes milk squirt from my tips. "Wow!" My voice is high-pitched as he catches my cream with his mouth, covering both my teats and guzzling my titty cream ravenously.

I need relief so bad. My pussy is on fire and I know Bryan is hard for me.

"I'm glad you're excited to be a part of our fashion

The Bully's Milky Roommate

house. Our HR department will give you an official call later in the day. I look forward to welcoming you on board."

Every suck of Bryan's lips is taking me higher. I know my panties are soaked and my pussy needs to swallow his cock to live.

"Yeah, sure....thanks a lot." I barely scrape five coherent words together before hanging up.

Throwing the phone away, I beg, "Bryan, please, I need you inside me right now."

My boyfriend pulls his wet lips off my tits, carrying me to bed with my legs hooked around his waist. He pushes me down and strips me bare before taking off his clothes. His veined, thick pole is ready and pulsing for me. I only breathe again when he spears me with his dick, sending me straight to heaven.

"Who was the phone call from?" he asks innocently, fucking me on the bed. His thrusts are hard and deep, scraping against my inner walls and making me see stars.

"A...fashion house I applied for...." I cling to him, fisting his hair as he sucks on my boobies. "My first choice." When he bites on my twin nipples, forcing me to hold them together for him, I cry out. My orgasm threatens to spill at any moment. The friction of his cock is driving me insane.

"What did they say?" he removes his mouth from me, riding me hard as his green gaze holds me captive. His dick is destroying my pussy, grinding against my sweet spot with every thrust.

"I made it!" I scream just as my climax sweeps over me.

"Good girl." Bryan's voice is distant as he continues fucking and milking me with wet sounds, taking me to paradise as a congratulatory gift. God, this is the most perfect moment in my life. A maelstrom of sensation drenches my senses as Bryan comes inside me after a few hard thrusts.

The feel of his hot cum filling me is divine. I want to be his wife, have his kids, and that whole New York life he dreams of. His fat cock plugs my pussy as I suck in his baby-making batter, wishing I could become pregnant right now.

When I open my eyes, he's looking at me, his cock twitching inside my pussy. I'm lying in a puddle of my own milk, my boyfriend's cock buried inside me, smiling like a lunatic. He makes me so happy.

"Congratulations, baby. I knew you could do it." He leans down, kissing my lips. "Should we go to the fancy Italian place in town to celebrate?"

I gaze at him through a shimmery film of tears, realizing how true his words are. Bryan was the only one who believed in me throughout this journey. He's the only one who cares about me. He knows sides of me that nobody does.

"I don't need a fancy dinner. My boyfriend's dick inside me is what I need."

"Baby, you're gonna get that every day." Bryan's lips meet mine and I loop my hand around his neck, kissing him back.

As our lips remain locked in a long kiss, a realization solidifies in my chest.

I'm in love with my roommate.

I'm in love with Bryan Livingston.

Chapter 6
Bryan

I gaze up at Katie, sweaty and panting after practice. My milky roommate is sitting on the bleachers, waiting for me. She usually watches me from afar, but having her close feels like admitting to the world that we're together.

"Will you stop staring at her?" Daniel, my teammate slams his palm on my shoulder. "You've been looking at Katie throughout practice. Are you sure she's just your roommate?"

I cough, unable to deny the feelings coursing through me. Katie and I have been making out every day and as time passes, our bond grows even stronger. When she told me she'd gotten an apprenticeship in New York, I decided to accept NYU's offer even though mom and dad were keen for me to go to Harvard. However, I want to be near my cupcake. She's my new addiction and I can't imagine my life without her anymore.

"It's weird to see you two getting along after you've been bullying her for years." Peter joins in. "I get that she's your roommate and ya'll need to make it work, but…it's just strange."

He shakes his head, disappearing from the field. I jog up to Katie who isn't smiling today. I wonder if she's okay.

"Hey." I can't stop a grin from spreading on my face at the sight of her. She's wearing a football team hoodie with my number, her deliciously thick legs clad in black tights. I reach out and smooth a lock of hair that's falling on her temple back.

"Hey." Her shy blue eyes look at me from under her thick lashes and it goes straight to my groin. "You were really good during practice. I think you're ready for the finals next week."

"You think so?" I tease. "Because the boys thought I was all distracted by the sight of you."

Katie blushes and I hate that she has to hold back her natural instinct to touch me. I want to wrap my arms around my sexy girlfriend's waist and kiss her without having to worry about who is watching.

"Are you coming to the game next week? I have VIP tickets for you."

"Of course. I'd never miss my boyfriend's game." She grins and I bend, needing to kiss her. However, when one of the boys emerges from the shower shouting his goodbyes to me, Katie backs away, panicking.

"Bye!" I wave to my teammate before telling my girlfriend. "I'll see you in the dorm. I need to shower."

"I'll wait," she says. "I have something to tell you."

Her words sound low, making me wonder if everything is all right. She has been sewing more than usual since she received that call but she didn't do any sewing yesterday. Katie told me she was going to tell her mom about the offer. I wonder how that went.

The Bully's Milky Roommate

I hurriedly jog into the showers, losing my clothes and letting the warm water run over my skin. When I'm done, the showers are empty. I walk out in just a towel, hoping to find my other teammates in the locker room, but it's already empty. Did I shower that long? The boys are usually eager to go to the dining hall after a long and sweaty practice session so the locker room clears out pretty fast after evening practice sessions.

I open my locker, ready to fish out my clothes, when I hear the locker room door open. My head swirls around, meeting Katie's gaze.

"Katie." My girlfriend walks into the locker room, checking around to make sure we're alone.

"Daniel told me you were alone." She walks toward me, worrying her lower lip with her teeth. I reach out and grab her, pushing her against the lockers as my hands wind around my girlfriend's lush hips. My lips are on hers before she can speak. Katie clothes her eyes, pushing her fingers into my wet hair as our mouths fuse together in an electric kiss. Her soft lips melt against mine, my bulge rubbing into her stomach. God, her sweet strawberry scent makes me so hard. She moans when her tits press against my hard chest, tilting her head to allow me deeper access. My tongue claims her mouth, tangling with hers and drinking her in. Our lips part, your hearts beating fast.

"I missed you." I am breathless, my eyes dark with desire. The team has been practicing more than usual because of the upcoming finals. That means I haven't gotten to spend as much time as I want with my cupcake.

"Me too." Her fingers caress my wet hair. "Seeing you makes me feel so much better."

I notice her frown and realize something is troubling

her. She's been looking more stressed than usual. "What's wrong, cupcake? Something's bothering you."

It's been three weeks since she got the apprenticeship at House of Accardo and she still hasn't told her parents about it. She also hasn't accepted the official offer yet, which tells me something is off. My hand drops to her, my thumb stroking the inside of her wrist. She has frown lines on her face.

"Baby, is this about telling your parents?" I kiss her lips when her frown deepens, trying to cheer her up. "I'm sure it's gonna go better than you think." She sighs. When she turns to me, her eyes appear a little glassy. My heart breaks. "What happened, cupcake?"

I don't know why, but I just want to see Katie happy. It's like she's my little pocket of sunshine. Seeing her look so excited when she comes up with a new design makes my day. I love supporting her and getting to be part of her journey. But the way she looks at me tells me something is wrong.

"I called my mom this morning." Her lips are trembling. "She...she's not happy about it. She thinks I should go to college."

I kiss her again, trying to calm her down. Katie lets me soothe her, kissing me back desperately. We both need each other and I'm only starting to realize how much.

"Maybe she just needs more time to adjust to your plan." I gaze at her swollen lips glistening and wet, making me want to take her against the lockers.

"It's bad, Bryan. Mom says she'll cut me off if I don't go to college and get a degree. I even considered getting a degree in fashion design, but mom said if I wanted to be employable, I needed to major in something more commercial."

"I'm so sorry, baby." I hold her closer, letting her rest her head on my chest. Her concern is palpable and I just want to make her feel better. I kiss her head, rubbing circles on her back.

"I think I'll try talking to dad next, but I don't expect him to be different. My parents have always had a fixed vision for my life and...I never thought how stifling that would become." I totally get her. My parents have my life planned out too. "Maybe I need to look into other options."

"That's not what you want, though." I remind her. "Designing clothes is your dream, not attending some stuffy Ivy League school on the East Coast."

"I don't have a choice, Bryan. I can't support myself if my parents cut me off."

"You have me." My words drop instantly like it's the most natural thing to say. I kiss her temple as she looks at me, stunned. "I'll support you."

"Bryan." Her lips part. "I...can't make you do that."

"Why not? I've got the money and since I'm eighteen, I can use some of my funds as I please."

"I can't live off my boyfriend. The apprenticeship pays a little bit, maybe I'll be able to make it work."

We both know she can't afford rent in New York City on how much her apprenticeship pays.

"We could move in together," I tell her. I've thought about it a lot. "I accepted NYU's offer. I'll be going to New York too. You could live in my house. I told you we've got a big house in New York City."

"That..." She knows living with me would help her out. "I thought you wanted to go to Harvard."

"My parents wanted me to go to Harvard. I just want to go wherever you are."

Jade Swallow

"Bryan..." Katie gazes up at me. "Are you sure? I don't want you to give up on your future plans because of me."

"You're my future plan, Katie. I'm going to make you my wife and support your dream, cupcake. Everything else in my life was planned by my parents. You're the only thing that's all mine." I kiss her nose, startling her.

"I...I never thought you'd be so serious about me. We've only been going out for a month and we aren't even official yet."

"If you want to be official, I can make us official," I tell her. "But I know what I want, Katie. A life with you is everything I've dreamed of. I can't let you go, baby." She inhales and exhales, her eyes filling up with tears again. "Are you crying?"

"No." Her voice is a little high-pitched. "It's just that...I never thought you'd fall for me, Bryan Livingston."

"I have fallen for you," I admit out loud. "And I don't ever want to go back."

She gets on her tiptoes and our lips meet again. The world is bright and full of color when I'm kissing the girl of my dreams. She and I are so good together.

"I just want you to be happy, Katie," I tell her as she reaches for the knot on my towel, horny after that long kiss. "After everything I put you through, you deserve to be happy. Just follow your dreams and let me worry about the rest, okay? I'm gonna take care of you, cupcake."

"I love you, Bryan," she says as the towel falls to the floor, exposing my thick, pulsing dick that's always hard for my girl. When she strokes my length with her fleshy fingers, I gasp. "I...I never thought I'd ever fall in love with you, but you're so kind and generous and hot and..." She sniffs. "I guess it just happened."

"It just happened for me too." I kiss her cheek. "You're

so easy to love, Katie. I want to see you grow and flourish in life. Just let me be by your side, okay?"

"Okay." Her stroking grows faster. She sinks to her knees, her kiss-swollen mouth lining up with my shaft. A bead of pre-cum forms on my tip. Katie shoots out her tongue and licks a circle around my sensitive tip." But first, I'm going to blow you."

"Damn it, baby." My fingers sink into her hair as she teases my tip with her tongue. When she wraps those juicy, wet lips around my cock, my core blazes like a furnace, aching to explode inside my girlfriend's mouth. She swallows me down inch by inch, her tongue licking the underside of my shaft and tracing my protruding veins. "God, Katie, you're a sex goddess."

She giggles around my shaft, the forbiddances of our encounter making us both hot. Anyone could walk into the locker room and find my girlfriend blowing me. But I'm too far gone to stop.

My hips begin to move as Katie's suction grows harder. My cock pistons in and out of her sexy little mouth, choking her when she deep throats me. I grab her hair and thrust into her sexy little mouth, feeling how her fleshy cheek walls clasp me. "Just like that, baby. You're doing so good."

Katie sucks and licks and tortures me, her fingers massaging and playing with my balls as I fuck her face harder. Her massive tits jiggle, her entire body shaking when my balls slap her chin, taking as much as she can give. The tip of my fat dick grinds against the roof of her mouth, pushing down the back of her throat and making her gag. Tears flow down her eyes, but she grabs my ass harder and blows me to a climax, never flinching.

The orgasm is inevitable. My entire body bursts into ribbons of joy, drenching her perfect mouth. She swallows it all down hungrily, making me come even harder. God, how did I get lucky enough to find such a perfect gem? My body disintegrates into waves of ecstasy and I ride them out with the love of my life.

Katie's lips are swollen and red when she finally spits out my wet, semi-soft dick several moments later. I let go of her hair and pull her up to her feet, kissing her cum-stained lips.

"I love you, Katie," I tell her. "I love you so damn much."

Chapter 7
Katie

"Good morning, baby." I wake up naked in bed with Bryan's hands wrapped around my waist. His cum has dried on my thighs, and my pussy is a little sore from being fucked by my hot boyfriend all night.

It's the day of his big match and I'm excited to see the team play. Bryan was nervous last night and couldn't sleep so we fucked to help him get the edge off. But we're so into each other that one orgasm turned into three and we kept going all night.

"Good morning." I turn around and Bryan presses his lips to me. I wrap my hand and legs around his body, feeling his morning wood press against my stomach as he kisses me. I love feeling him close to me. I love the intimacy we share. With him next to me, I feel that I can do anything.

My wet tips leak milk and I moan when they begin to hurt. Bryan's hands are immediately on my breasts, cupping and massaging them to start the flow of my milk. His deep green eyes gaze at me, his lips trailing down my jaw to my tits. When he presses a kiss on my wet nipple, I arch my hips needily. My legs open wide, needing my boyfriend's big cock between them.

"Did you sleep well last night?" he asks as his mouth finds one teat and latches on.

"Yeah." I lose myself to the sensation of his hot mouth suckling my cream and reliving my ache. I'm so damn addicted to being milked by my roommate. I hold him close, rubbing my wet pussy all over his dick. Every suck is hypnotic, making my pussy leak like a faucet until I'm dying to feel him inside me.

"Bryan...I need you." My moans get his attention, making him let go of my nipple.

"What's that, sweetie? You want my cock?" He pushes the blunt, engorged head of his dick between my legs. He's so hard and wet in the morning that I love it when he fucks me raw.

"Yeah," I admit, kissing his hair. "I'm always hungry for my boyfriend's cock."

"Good thing I love your pussy so much." He pushes into me, stretching me good. I cry out as his thickness fills me, making my pussy pulse with need. Bryan latches onto my other teat and guzzles my milk. My body is wet with trails of milk dripping down my breasts and Bryan's cock squelching in and out of my sopping hole.

"Yes, more..." I cry out as he rails me hard on our bed. We soundproofed the room after we started fucking so that our neighbors couldn't hear us and I take full advantage of that fact by screaming as loud as I want. My hands grab the headrail of the bed, my body moving with Bryan's every deep thrust. The friction flames the spark inside me until my pussy is spasming around his dick. "Bryan!"

I ignite with my lover's name on my lips. Bliss descends upon me, claiming my entire body.

The Bully's Milky Roommate

"Come for me, baby, just like that." Bryan's cock plumbs the depths of my pussy, scraping my sweet spot when he climaxes inside me. His loud grunt matches my screams as his balls explode, filling me up with his warm baby-making seed. My soul soars as we come into union, carried by the wings of pleasure. My pussy milks his cock, sucking in his seed like a needy slut. Sometimes when he breeds me, I wish this were real. I wish I could really have his kids and be his right now. There's nothing more perfect than when we come together.

The phone begins ringing just as I open my eyes. Rays of sunlight prickle my eyes and with a groan, I reach for the phone, my boyfriend still moving inside me. He kisses me as I see the name on the screen.

It's Saumya.

Dread fills the pit of my stomach that's still warm with Bryan's cum.

"Who's that, baby?" He sees her name too and frowns. "Answer it. I'm here with you."

I let him kiss my face as I answer the call.

The three-month mark is almost over and I'm worried Saumya will tell me we can't be roommates anymore. At first, that idea was so appealing. But then, I fell in love with Bryan. I love getting to sleep with him, to kiss him whenever I want, and be next to him. I never thought I'd grow so addicted to his presence but his cocky confidence is the perfect complement to my neuroticism and self-doubt. I love him so much and even though I know we'll continue seeing each other, I don't want us to be apart.

"Hello?" I swallow my demons, answering the phone.

"Hey, Katie, this is Saumya." The familiar voice makes goosebumps break over my skin. Bryan's hand strokes my hip, his eyebrows rising.

"Yeah?"

"I just wanted to let you know that a new spot has opened up in the boys' dorm. If Bryan wants to move out—"

"Can we stay roommates?" The words burst out of my mouth. "I mean, we've gotten used to each other, and with the exams coming up, it's going to be difficult to adjust to a new roommate." Bryan looks at me and I smile. "I was wondering if we could continue being roommates for the rest of the year."

"Are you sure?" Saumya asks. "I thought you wanted him gone."

"Umm...we've become friends," I tell her. "I think I'll be fine."

"If that's what you want, there are other students on the waitlist for a room. I can't assure you Bryan will get another chance to move out if he misses out on this one."

"That's fine." Bryan's voice cuts in. "I don't want to move out either." There's a wide grin on his face. "I told my mom that I wanted to be roommates with Katie for the rest of the year."

I raise my eyebrow, surprised his mom knows about me.

"Bryan." Saumya pauses. "In that case, I'll have the room reassigned to the first person on the waitlist. Thanks, guys."

"No problem," Bryan says before I hang up.

There's a moment of silence after the call. Bryan pulls out of me, coming to rest next to me. I turn and fall into his arms, gazing up at him. "You told your mom you wanted to be roommates with me?"

"Yeah. I wasn't going to let you go after that amazing blow job." He winks. "Besides, I'm too into you right now to even spend a moment away from you. You're my forever, Katie."

The Bully's Milky Roommate

Butterflies soar in my heart at his words.

Forever.

It seems like such a long period of time, yet, when Bryan says it, I know every day with him is going to be good. The future is no longer a bleak, black hole. Instead, it's a collection of joyful moments we're yet to experience together.

"So, we're gonna be roommates for the rest of the year?" I ask, my heart giddy with excitement. "Once upon a time, that was my greatest nightmare but right now, it feels like a dream come true."

"You're my dream come true, Katie," he says. "I love you, cupcake."

I revel in the feeling of being kissed by my boyfriend until the alarm rings again. With a groan, I push him off me, rolling off the bed.

"Are you ready for today's game?" I ask as I strut naked to the shower. Bryan follows me, his dick covered in my juices.

"Yeah, sleeping with you last night really helped." He winks as he turns on the shower and lets the water cover us both. I love showering together with my boyfriend every day. It makes me feel so connected and treasured.

"Do you even have any energy left to play football after fucking your girlfriend all night?" I chide, grabbing the shower gel.

"Baby, you're my recharge button. Fucking you gives me energy." He kisses me before spreading the body wash all over me. He soaps himself up and lets me run the shower.

"You're so cute when you're in love, Bryan." I kiss his cheek. Gazing into my boyfriend's loving eyes is my new favorite hobby.

* * *

The football field is packed. Cheerleaders do their routines as the team gazes at the scoreboard, sweaty and tired. There's less than one minute to go before the game ends.

I watch Bryan run with the football in his hand. The ticket he gave me granted me a first-row seat. My heart is in my throat as the final countdown begins. We just need one more goal to beat the opposing team and it's all in Bryan's hands. I pray for him, closing my eyes. I can't even see the last bit. That's how nervous I am.

"Touchdown!"

My eyes burst open when the announcer says the words I've been waiting to hear.

I tip my head up, drowning in the screams and cheers of fans. Bryan stands up, grinning as his teammates run across the field and lift him up, bellowing with joy. The scoreboard changes and Heathcliff's name dominates the display.

"And for the first time in two decades, Heathcliff Academy has made history by winning the golden cup."

The announcer's voice is lost amidst the screaming of fans. I stand up and scream with joy, wearing my boyfriend's jersey. My hoodie comes off and I proudly show off Bryan's number. I stole a spare jersey this morning because I wanted him to know that I was supporting him.

Bryan's gaze meets mine, his grin turning to surprise when he sees me wearing his jersey. The cheerleaders begin their routine and I race to the edge of the field. He gets off his teammates's shoulders and stalks toward me. The camera follows the star quarterback as he makes his way to the audience. People thrust out their hands to touch his, but he has eyes only for me. I stop waving the team flag, stunned at his open display of affection.

Bryan climbs up and for a moment, I'm caught by surprise. My heart beats in slow motion as he comes toward

The Bully's Milky Roommate

me, six feet of muscle and joy. I can't even move because when I look at him, I'm reminded of how much I love him.

He grabs me in a bear hug, much to everyone's shock. His teammates are staring, a moment of silence filling the stadium. Bryan's green eyes meet mine, his mouth quirking up in a smile. "You wore my jersey."

"Yeah, I wanted to support my boyfriend."

"So, we're official now?" His masculine scent is filling me up with need.

"I mean, you're standing in front of me and the cameras are pointed at us. I think that means we're official." It's like a movie.

He grins. "Why don't we seal it with a kiss, cupcake?"

"Lead the way."

His lips are on mine the next second. Cheers explode and the screen fills up with our faces, but I don't even care as I close my eyes and kiss my boyfriend in front of the whole world. Cheers fill the stadium again. Nobody expected him to be in love with me, but other people's opinions don't matter. I'm in love with my bully. My roommate. The best man I've met in my life. It's his love that I feel when he kisses me and holds me close.

"I love you, baby." Bryan is panting when he breaks the kiss. "I think I'm officially in love with my milky roommate. You're the sweetest part of my life, cupcake."

I don't let him go, feeling the applause wash over us. "I love you too, Bryan Livingston. You're the best thing that ever happened to me."

And then, we kiss again, giving the fans what they came here for. I think my final year is going to be pretty great.

Chapter 8
Bryan
Ten years later—

I watch proudly from the first row of Katie Livingston's fifth-year anniversary fashion show. It's a visual extravaganza. My wife has outdone herself again. Though I've been coming to her fashion shows for five years, I'm awed anew every time she launches a new collection.

It's been ten years since we got married and those have been the best ten years of my life. Katie and I had a lot of fun during the final year of high school. By the time we got to college, I was way too addicted to waking up next to her. We moved into an apartment together and Katie married me straight out of high school. I wasn't ready to wait for her to be mine, not when I knew she was the one. Her parents finally came around, but by them, she was my wife. Katie flourished in New York and after five years with House of Accardo, she launched her own brand, Katie Livingston. Thanks to its inclusive designs and a focus on originality, the brand grew and grew and I've more than quadrupled my original investment. Not that I care about making

The Bully's Milky Roommate

money back. Getting to see Katie live her dream is all I need.

I work for the Livingston family now as the director of the New York branch. However, my priority is always going to be my stunning wife who makes me happy every day. My parents were shocked when I first declared that I wanted to marry Katie right out of high school. However, they really liked her when they met her, so they came around soon enough. We were married in a grand ceremony three months after she began her apprenticeship. My parents Katie is the best decision I ever made since they get to have a successful fashion designer for a daughter-in-law.

My wife walks onto the stage, looking like a queen in that sexy blue dress that she first designed when we were in high school. Not even the generous skirt is enough to hide her seven-month-old baby bump that she proudly shows off to the world. Models of all sizes and body types cluster around my radiant wife, spreading the message of body positivity to the world.

I clap, giving my wife a standing ovation for her newest collection.

"Thank you to everyone who came to our fifth-anniversary show." Her soft voice makes everyone go silent. I love it when she shines on stage. "Katie Livingston is now one of the biggest inclusive couture brands in America and we just got the French Ministry of Industry's Haute Couture designation, marking a new high for our brand." There is applause from members of the audience, many of whom are A-list celebrities, influencers, and top journalists and fashion buyers. "It's a special show for me because I'm going to be a mom soon." She caresses her baby bump and I feel sparks in my heart. "A lot of people played an integral part in my journey. I'd like to thank Maria Accardo from the House of Accardo for being the best mentor I could've asked for. I wouldn't have been able to create such detailed designs without her mentorship." She breathes, letting the pause sit. "However, there is someone without whom this journey wouldn't have been possible. And that's my husband Bryan. Thank you, Bryan, for being my first and most ardent supporter. Without you, I never would've found the courage to come to New York and make my dreams come true. You believed in me before anyone else did. I love you so much."

I blow kisses to my wife, my heart swelling. She's so beautiful and talented and I always want her light to shine bright in the world. The whole audience applauds for my wife and I watch as she soaks up the limelight. I can't wait to get back home and shower her with my love.

* * *

The moment we return from the fashion show, Katie and I are on each other. We stumble in through the door of our Upper East Side townhouse, kissing each other feverishly. She's been busy for the last two days, trying to put the finishing touches on her show and that means I haven't gotten the opportunity to milk and rail my wife.

I reach for the zipper at the back of her bodice and pull it down, letting her milky breasts fall free. "Ever since I saw you in that dress, I've been wanting to get it off." I kiss her swollen breasts that are encased in a beige nursing bra. She wears this dress for our anniversary every year. It's our special moment. "I can't believe you wore our dress to your fifth anniversary."

The Bully's Milky Roommate

"I wanted to wear a special dress for a special day." He plants a peck on my lips, gazing at me with those liquid blue eyes. I push her dress off her shoulders, leaving my pregnant wife in nothing but her bra and panties. My breath stops as I gaze at the most beautiful woman in the world.

My palms slide over her heavy, swollen belly, groaning when she caresses my hair. I sink to my knees, running my hot lips over her pregnant stomach. "You look so beautiful all swollen and big with our babies, cupcake. You have no idea how long I've wanted to see you like this."

After we got married, we decided to wait before having kids. With Katie's new job at the fashion house and my college degree, we were busy all the time. So, we decided to just enjoy life by ourselves for some time. However, last year, Katie said she was ready to start trying. I was so glad to finally get to breed my wife without any protection. Those were the best two months of my life. When the test came out positive just weeks later, none of us were surprised.

"Mmmm...Being bred by you is the best feeling ever," she says, caressing my head as I kiss every inch of that delectable baby bump. Watching my curvy wife in her most fertile form is a different kind of drug. "I've wanted to carry your babies since high school."

Katie and I are having twins. We found out a few weeks ago when we went to the doctor. I'm so excited to become a dad for the first time, but I also want to make sure my wife remains my priority and her needs are always met.

"Lay down, Mrs. Livingston." I escort my pregnant wife to bed. I strip down as she lays on the soft mattress, her big belly pointing up. When I'm down to my boxers, I climb into bed, pulling her leg into my lap and massaging her swollen feel. Thanks to her pregnancy, she's all swollen.

"It must've been hard being on your feet for so long," I tell her. "Baby, you were stunning tonight. I don't even know how you do it. It's like you get better every time you launch a collection."

"I couldn't have done it without you, Mr. Livingston," she says, enjoying being pampered, when I move on to her other foot, she moves her leg, teasing the contours of my bulge with her toes. "Mmm...now come to bed and make love to your pregnant wife."

"Are you wet already, Mrs. Livingston?" I shoot her a heated look and she thrusts out her breasts.

"I'm engorged, husband." She reaches for the front clasp of her bra and pulls it off. Her two melon-sized tits jump out, the saucer-sized tips fat and filled with juicy cream. My cock jumps into action, teased by her toes and the sight of those ripe, milky tits. After high school, Katie stopped lactating. I enjoy her curvy body, nevertheless, but when she began producing milk again a few weeks ago, I knew I didn't want to kiss a single moment of it.

"Damn, you're tempting, cupcake." My wife smiles as her bra falls off. I reach down and push her panties away, opening her legs to take a look at her ripe, pink pussy that's all wet and swollen.

"Baby, you're my favorite dessert." I push my face between her legs, licking her slit. Her delicate folds quiver at my touch, leaking more honey on my tongue. I tease her silken folds before my mouth wraps around her hard, tiny clit. When I suck on it, milk fountains from her massive tits, flowing down her belly and right into my mouth. "Mmm..the taste of your milk with your pussy is divine." I lap up her cream and honey suckling and teasing her little bud until she's begging me to take her.

The Bully's Milky Roommate

"Please, Bryan, I need your cock."

With the taste of her pussy in my mouth, I back off, licking my lips. "On your hands and feet, cupcake."

She obeys instantly, looking like the most delicious sight in the world as she goes on all fours, offering that big, sexy ass to me. Her heavy stomach hangs low, her engorged tits dripping milk like cow udders.

"Gosh, baby, you're so gorgeous when you're all pregnant and milky. I want to keep you knocked up forever." My big hands cup her breasts, gently teasing those aroused nipples with my thumbs. She moans in response, extra sensitive thanks to her pregnancy. "I love your curvy body. Pregnancy looks so good on you." I gently knead and milk her breasts like cow udders, watching milk drip onto the bedsheets. I'm going to drink from her titties later. My milk-coated hands trail down her big belly, massaging her.

Then, without warning, I spear her pussy with my cock, feeling her entire body clench.

"Oh god, Bryan...you're so big." I fill her up, plugging that pregnant pussy with my dick until my wife is shaking all over, screaming my name. I begin thrusting into her, drowning in the wet, welcoming heat of her juicy cunt. My hands touch all over her big belly, sinking into her curvy hips as heat shoots up my groin.

I drive deep into her, pulling out and slamming in hard. "Baby, you look so sexy with those fat udders and big stomach bouncing." The way her pussy wraps around me makes my brain short-circuit. "I love railing you when you're pregnant, Mrs. Livingston. I've wanted to fuck you raw when you're swollen with my baby ever since high school."

"Mmmm...you give the best orgasms, Mr. Livingston. I

love how you take care of my needs during my pregnancy." My cock squelches in and out of her hole, teasing her sweet spot and increasing fiction. My balls slap against her ass as I drill her cunt hard, feeling my orgasm shimmering so close. Katie's fingers clutch the bedsheets and when I feel her pussy squeeze my dick, I know she's going to come.

"Bryan!" My wife and I explode at the same time, the colossal force of a double orgasm knocking me off the center. My cock grinds hard and deep into her fertilized womb and explodes into ribbons of hot cum.

"God, I love breeding you so much, baby. Just stuffing your fertile pussy with cum makes my day."

"Mmm..." She cries out. "It feels so good when I'm filled with your seed."

Our bodies spasm and soar, riding out the twin orgasms together. My hands steady her stomach, kissing her back, her neck, and her hair as she comes for me over and over again.

Moments later, I lay on my wife's big stomach, suckling cream from her full breasts as she caresses my hair. She's going to be such a good mother. Katie is kind and nurturing and just her presence brings me so much comfort. Her sweet cream flows into my mouth, reviving me. I lick and suck her squishy nipple, bringing her pleasure as we enjoy a moment of quiet after an intense orgasm.

"I love you," she tells me, lowering her head to press a kiss onto my temple. "I'm so glad you were assigned to be my roommate that year. If you hadn't found me milking in the bathroom, we'd never have this wonderful life. Being my bully's milky roommate really changed my life."

"Mmm...baby, I like to think I'd have found you anywhere in the world." I plop her wet nipple out, my lips sliding over her wet tip. "But you're right. I'm glad I finally

The Bully's Milky Roommate

realized that you were too precious to lose. I'm never going to let you go, Katie. You're my everything." I raise my head, my fingers teasing her belly. "I love you, cupcake."

Our lips meet in a long, hot kiss. With my curvy wife by my side, life's only going to get better.

About the Author

Jade Swallow is an author of super steamy novels. She loves reading and writing filthy tales featuring all kinds of kinks. Follow her on Instagram @authorjadeswallow for news about upcoming books.

Sign up for my newsletter here to get updates about my upcoming releases: subscribepage.io/eiSMM1

Also by Jade Swallow

Want to read more books in the Dark Fantasies series?

Milkmaid for my Bully: A dark high school milking fantasy with pregnancy

My Tutor, My Stalker: A dark high school stalker romance with milking and pregnancy

Miked by my Ex's Older Brother: A forbidden age gap hucow milking fantasy with pregnancy

Love Daddy kink, breeding, and milking? Check out these books:

Breeding the Babysitter: A forbidden age gap billionaire romance with pregnancy (Forbidden Daddies #1)

Mountain Daddy's Curvy Maid : A grumpy-sunshine age gap romance with pregnancy and lactation (Mountain Daddies #1)

Pregnant by the Mafia Boss : A forbidden age gap mafia romance with pregnancy (Mafia Daddies #1)

Lessons in Love with my Brother's Best Friend: A forbidden age gap erotica with pregnancy and BBW milking

Milked by my Best Friend's Mom : An age gap lesbian erotic novella

Looking for paranormal and omegaverse erotica? Check out these books by me:

The Vampire's Milkmaid: A gothic fated mates billionaire vampire romance with breeding, milking, and pregnancy (Paranormal Mates #1)

Stranded on the Shifter's Mountain: A Fated Mates Werewolf Shifter Romance with Breeding and Pregnancy (Paranormal Mates #2)

A Hucow Nanny for the Alpha Daddies: An age gap reverse harem fated mates omegaverse novella with pregnancy and milking (Omegaverse Daddies #1)

Alpha Daddy's Omega: An age gap pregnancy knotting and pregnant short story with arranged marriage (Omegaverse Daddies #2)

The Sea God's Fertile Bride : An age gap tentacle monster erotica (Married and Pregnant Monster Shorts #1)

Beauty and the Orc: An age gap orc daddy monster romance (Married and Pregnant Monster Shorts #2)

Short story bundles with milking, age gap, and breeding:

Summer Heat Series Bundle (Summer Heat #1-5)

Feeding Fantasies Box Set (Feeding Fantasies 1-5 + 2 bonus shorts)

Creamy and Pregnant Short Stories (Billionaires & Hucows #1-5)

Creamy Fantasies Box Set (Creamy Fantasies #1-5)

Looking for more dark and steamy college-age romances by me? Check out this one:

Broken (Twisted Souls #1)

She's a serial killer on a mission, and he's her next target. But things get complicated when she begins falling for him.

Printed in Great Britain
by Amazon